"I'm not interested in one-night stands."

Adam's arrogance brought a tide of color to Anna's smooth cheeks. She had imagined it might be interesting to get to know him, but that didn't mean she'd intended to jump into bed with him! "Don't you think your moral superiority is hypocritical when you've been privately lusting after me since you walked into the room?"

"Everything you do screams sex! The dress, the way you move...."

"This is a party. I came prepared to enjoy myself," Anna replied.

"I'd noticed." Adam took her face in his hands and tasted the sweet moistness of her mouth. Later he'd have leisure to regret his action, but at that moment all he was aware of was an intense hunger....

Wanted: three husbands for three sisters!

Anna, Lindy and Hope—triplet sisters and the best, the closest, of friends. Physically, these three women may look alike: but their personalities are very different! Anna is lively and vivacious, Lindy is the practical one and Hope sparkles with style and sophistication.

But they have one thing in common: each sister is about to meet a man she will tantalize, torment and finally tame! And when these spirited women find true love, they'll become the most beautiful triplet brides....

Turn the page to enjoy Anna's story in
Wild and Willing!

And look out for:

The Secret Father on sale in March 2000
(Harlequin Presents® #2096)
An Innocent Affair in June 2000
(Harlequin Presents® #2114)

KIM LAWRENCE

Wild and Willing!

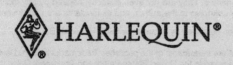

TORONTO • NEW YORK • LONDON
AMSTERDAM • PARIS • SYDNEY • HAMBURG
STOCKHOLM • ATHENS • TOKYO • MILAN • MADRID
PRAGUE • WARSAW • BUDAPEST • AUCKLAND

ISBN 0-373-12078-8

WILD AND WILLING!

First North American Publication 2000.

Visit us at www.romance.net

Printed in U.S.A.

CHAPTER ONE

ADAM DEACON turned his head to watch the progress of the young woman on the dance floor. He considered himself too old to be interested in such a child, but he doubted he was the only male present unable to take his eyes from her supple, rhythmic contortions. Each sinuously sensual movement of her slight frame echoed the heavy throb of the popular tune the band was playing.

'Want to dance?' his companion asked, watching his absorption with a speculative smile.

'Not my sort of dance.' He switched his attention. Rosalind was intelligent and beautiful, and he hadn't heard a thing she'd said for several minutes. She was also far too astute to miss this embarrassing fact, but too polite to mention it. It was one of the qualities that made her a great companion.

'Good, isn't she?' Rosalind murmured.

Adam didn't pretend to misunderstand her. 'You know the wild child?' His green eyes flickered in the direction of the young woman just in time to see her throw her arms around her partner's neck and kiss him on the mouth. The music had ended, and she smilingly ignored several entreaties to continue.

'Wild child!' Rosalind Lacey gave a laugh. 'How appropriate,' she said with a grin. 'Yes, you could say I know her.' She gave a secret smile.

The music had stopped and she gestured to the girl who waved back and began to weave her way through the throng of revellers. 'I'll introduce you.'

Adam wasn't pleased. Whilst he might have been entertained by the abandoned performance, his interest didn't extend further. He had never understood why mature men were attracted to young girls with undeveloped personalities. He had no wish to meet a teenager with an exhibitionist streak. The thought of laboured conversation made him frown before his expression turned politely bland as the slender brunette approached.

Closer to, he could see she wasn't beautiful. Her features were not as perfectly proportioned as her lissom body. The masterful nose and full mouth were too big for her small oval face. It was the eyes that captured attention. Wide-spaced, warm brown and slanted like a fawn's, they were fringed by extravagant dark lashes. There was, however, none of that creature's coyness in the direct gaze.

'Are you all right, Anna?' Rosalind asked anxiously. It was rare to see any external evidence of her sister's old injury, an injury that had tragically halted a promising career as a ballet dancer.

Adam's keen, professional eyes had also noted the way the girl was placing most of her weight on one leg. He automatically looked at her legs; not much was concealed from his eyes in the short black dress she wore. It was a scrap of fabric that moulded the thrust of her small, high breasts and flared slightly at the hemline, which was very high. He couldn't see any visible sign of injury in the slim, shapely line of her legs through their black fine denier covering; they looked in remarkably good shape!

'Don't fuss,' Anna replied with impatient good humour.

Adam raised his gaze to find the remarkable pair of dark brown eyes, still shining with exhilaration after her performance, watching him with amusement and not a trace of self-consciousness.

'You'll recognise them again,' she observed with a straight face, stretching one elegant ankle in front of her.

'You were limping,' he accused, just to rectify any

wrong ideas she might have about his interest. Her poise was precocious even at a time when childhood grew ever shorter.

'It's not usually noticeable. Before you say it, Lindy, dear, I know I shouldn't have danced like that, but it was worth it! I love that tune.' She gave a blissful sigh.

'Ever heard of moderation?' Rosalind asked her sister with rueful affection.

She knew she was wasting her breath; Anna was a creature of extremes. Sometimes she envied her sister her lack of inhibitions, but mostly she worried that Anna's spontaneity might lead people to miss the sensitivity inherent in her sister's personality. The total lack of artifice made her seem frighteningly vulnerable to the more cautious Rosalind.

'Ever heard of death by boredom?' Anna's attention flicked to the tall, silent man at Lindy's side. 'Either you're a gatecrasher or Lindy brought you. I wrote the invitations personally,' she explained, looking him up and down with a candid interest that brought a flicker of disapproval to his eyes.

'Anna, this is Adam Deacon. Adam, this is Anna, my sister.'

'You mean there are more of you? I'd have thought your parents would have called it a day after triplets. They must be gluttons for punishment!'

'Don't you like children, Mr Deacon?' Anna enquired.

'In moderation.'

'He sounds like just your sort of man, Lindy,' she mocked gently. Rosalind, with her soft, honey-coloured hair and serene blue eyes, never lost her cool. Anna hoped her sister would one day meet a man who would shake that equilibrium. Was this the man? If so she would have to keep her fantasies to herself.

Rosalind glared discouragingly; Anna's offbeat sense of humour could be provocative when she chose.

'Adam is to be the new orthopaedic consultant at St

Jude's,' she explained. 'He's not my man,' she added with an apologetic smile in Adam's direction. 'I thought it might be nice if he got to know a few people locally. There are only the three of us, Adam; Anna is the eldest, despite appearances.'

'My apologies,' he said, startled by this information. He knew Rosalind was twenty-six, but this provocative creature could have passed for a teenager.

'I was the runt,' Anna said.

'So I see.'

Anna's eyes widened. 'That wasn't very kind.'

For someone who was meant to be meeting people, he had an aloof air which was pretty daunting. Did a warm, interesting man lurk beneath the austere exterior? Was the gleam in his eyes humour? She hoped so. It would be a great waste if he turned out to be a beautiful stuffed shirt. He *was* beautiful, though, she conceded.

'You don't appear to need your confidence bolstered.'

That, he decided, was a considerable understatement. She had none of the quiet reticence of her sister, who was, he'd always thought, a very serene woman. There was nothing covert about the sexuality the brunette oozed, either. Without intending to his eyes dropped to skim over the sleek slenderness of her slight frame.

'You dance well.' He recalled her undulations across the dance floor and felt a distinct tightness around his collar.

Anna shivered. She'd known he was watching her from across the room, but closer to the scrutiny didn't just send her pulse racing—it made her stomach muscles go into a series of spasms and her throat grow dry.

He had been hard to miss, even in this crowded rom. He was lean and tall, several inches over six feet, with dull gold hair that gleamed under the electric lights. He was the sort of person who made an impact the instant he walked into a room, and his long-limbed grace had captured and held her imagination.

She'd told herself he was probably cross-eyed, or a martyr to acne, but closer inspection had revealed he was neither. Closer to, the air of confidence and authority was more pronounced, as was the fluid, feral manner in which he moved. His eyes were a mysterious green and his skin was faintly tanned; if you added the firm mouth and aquiline nose you had, in short, perfection! If you were the sort of person who was impressed by such things.

She, of course, was not so shallow and superficial, but she was human enough to feel quite pleased when her sister denied ownership of this superb specimen. She wondered if she would ever feel enough for a man to put him above her relationship with her sisters. She doubted it.

'Can you dance?' she teased.

'With less abandon than you.'

'I can adapt.'

'Are you asking me to dance?'

'Should I have waited for you to ask me?' She gave him a tiny smile and tilted her head on one side in a gesture that revealed the swan-like arch of her neck, and made Adam's better judgement die an instant death. He'd left recklessness behind years ago, along with his impulsive youth, but somehow he found himself too intrigued to back down from the challenge in her provocative manner.

'You think I was going to?' The crackle of awareness that passed between them was almost physical in its strength. The startled flash in her wide eyes revealed she too had felt the sensation.

Anna wasn't about to disintegrate into coy confusion at this point, despite her accelerated heart rate and the quiet but growing conviction she was making a fool of herself.

'When the music was in keeping with your dignity I thought you might work yourself up to it.'

'You think I have dignity?' His mouth lifted in a satirical curve as his eyes smiled, almost reluctantly, back at her.

'God, does he always ask this many questions?' Anna demanded of her silent sister. 'I think your dignity is awesome,' she told him gravely. 'I'm sure you have the nurses fluttering around you to obey your every whim.'

'You have a very old-fashioned idea of the doctor-nurse relationship,' he observed with a sardonic twist to his lips.

'That's me—an old-fashioned girl.'

'How appropriate—a waltz for an old-fashioned girl.'

Rosalind watched them move away with a sharp frown of concern. She hadn't failed to notice the inexplicable electricity that had flared between her sister and Adam Deacon. She'd been breathless just listening to the lightning exchanges. But it was the silent communication of their bodies and eyes that worried her most. How could she warn Anna without playing the interfering sister? There was a delicate balance between sisterly concern and interference.

He really could dance, which was the first pleasant surprise for Anna. The second was the effect that being held in close proximity to him had on her nervous system. The quivers of sensation that rippled through her entire body made her forget the tiresome ache in her knee. All the couples on the darkened floor were entwined to some extent, so she could legitimately appreciate the hardness of her partner's lean, muscled frame.

'You dance very well, Adam.' She raised her head to look up at him. She was intrigued by the angles and planes of his face and puzzled by his sardonic expression which bordered on disapproval.

'Are you always so…*friendly*, Miss Lacey?' He gave the word an unpleasant connotation. Dancing might be an innocent enough pursuit, but he had discovered that it was less so when partnering this disturbing young woman. What the hell am I doing? he asked himself angrily.

'You're here to meet the locals,' Anna pointed out, unwittingly answering his silent question.

Recognising the sudden quality of harsh hostility that had been in his voice made her smile falter, and the feeling of heady expectation dissipated. There was no redeeming humour behind his abrupt shift in mood. She had been experiencing the strangest feeling that she was embarking on one of the great adventures in her life, and she was a great one for following gut instinct on such matters. It seemed she'd been wrong.

'I'm a local. But, if you danced with me out of politeness, don't worry, I'll let you go now. I thought you wanted to dance.' She began to detach her hands, which had lain against his chest, but he moved one of his own hands from around her waist and restrained them.

'I did want to. I'm just not used to women who take the lead. I like to do the asking.'

His voice was like rich, bitter chocolate and it made her give a tiny sigh of appreciation. Stuffed shirt with a macho inclination, she thought sadly; what a waste!

'I think it's a very good thing you're not my sister's boyfriend.'

'You draw the line at seducing your siblings' lovers? I think I should make it clear so you don't waste any more of your time—I'm not interested in one-night stands.'

Seduce! His condescending arrogance made her chin jut aggressively and brought a fresh tide of colour to her smooth cheeks. If he couldn't handle candour and honesty that was his problem. She found him attractive, and didn't see why she should hide the fact. She had imagined it might be interesting to get to know him. But that hadn't meant she intended jumping into bed with him.

'As a matter of fact I think Lindy needs someone to bring out her more relaxed, less proper side. You're far too repressed and grim for her...possibly for anyone,' she mused silkily, staring pointedly at the long, strong fingers wrapped around her wrists.

Adam Deacon looked startled and then angry as the purring kitten in his arms turned into an angry cat. He'd intended to subdue the waves of sultry invitation she was emanating—as much for his sake as her own—not anger her.

'A little repression, not to mention discrimination, might do *you* some good. Your sister is a fine doctor with an excellent future. Perhaps you should try and emulate her decorum.'

The pompous... She inhaled angrily and gritted her teeth. 'Decorum!' she hooted. 'I like Miss Austen as much as the next person, but I prefer living in this century when women's lives aren't dependent on men! First impressions are a constant source of disappointment to me,' she bemoaned.

His first impression of *her* was obviously that she was some sort of promiscuous slut, and his anxiety not to be contaminated by her was embarrassingly obvious.

'Tell me, Doctor, was your personality bypass a surgical procedure, or is it congenital? Don't you find it a tad hypocritical to come down with a dose of moral superiority when you've been privately lusting after me since you walked into the room?'

'I think you're the sort of female who is only happy when every male within shouting distance is lusting after you,' he returned scornfully. 'Everything you do screams sex!'

That scalding accusation really threw her. 'That's ridiculous!' She'd always worked on the premise that what people saw was what they got where she was concerned. It had never occurred to her that anyone would see *that*!

'The dress.' His eyes regarded one shoestring strap that had slipped over her shoulder. 'The way you move… It's all a come-on, and not a very subtle one at that.'

'This is a party; I came prepared to enjoy myself.' He lifted his fingers from her bare skin as if he'd been stung, and she wondered if he'd felt the same electrical prickle she had.

'I'd noticed,' he bit back, his lip curling with distaste.

'The music's stopped; you hadn't noticed *that*,' she said, smiling with sweet insincerity into his grim face.

She saw him realise that they'd been standing immobile in the middle of the floor, which was now clearing, making them even more conspicuous. He cast her a look of disgust and mumbled something rude under his breath.

When she turned to go he was at her side. 'Feeling the magnetic draw of my personality?' She headed for the terrace door.

She needed fresh air! God, what a let-down this man had been, she thought, furious that she'd let her imagination endow the perfect frame with an equally ideal personality.

'Stalking off in the opposite direction would make us look even more conspicuous.'

'But I thrive on notoriety,' she drawled sarcastically.

'Notorious doctors rarely advance professionally.'

'You didn't look interesting enough to be classed as notorious, just silly.'

'I'm repressed *and* silly, am I?' he said grimly. When she shrugged he spun her round to face him, placing one hand in the small of her back.

'You're probably too old to change now,' she observed sympathetically. 'Some woman like boringly predictable men.'

'You really are…!' With a sound of anger rumbling in his throat he took her face in his hands and plunged into the sweet moistness of her mouth. Later, he'd have the leisure to regret his action, but at the moment all he was aware of was an intense hunger.

Shock at this reprisal of her antagonistic jibe held Anna completely immobile for a frozen moment. Slowly it filtered through to her that the instinctive rejection she'd been relying on wasn't going to materialise. He was demanding a response from her and, whilst she ought to have been repelled by this ruthless onslaught, she only experienced an urgent, compelling desire to give him everything he was asking for.

Senses awake like never before, she was bombarded with a myriad of impressions—the taste of his mouth, warm and fragrant, the heavy thud of his heartbeat and the impression of one hard thigh thrust between her own legs. She clutched at him because her knees showed a tendency to shake. And it wasn't just her knees; her entire body was vibrating as a tide of heat raised her temperature several degrees. Standing on tiptoes, her slender body stretched in an arc, she could just place her hands around his neck.

With a husky groan he placed both hands on her waist and physically put her from him. She took several gulps of air and tried to steady her laboured breathing. Adam was staring at her as if she had two heads. His narrowed eyes gleamed with a very uncomplimentary mixture of horror and disgust.

'You accused *me* of being unsubtle,' Anna said huskily. Her flippancy was a cover for her confusion. The kiss, delivered solely in a spirit of frustrated retribution, had shaken her to the core.

She smoothed her sleek, short hair back into shape, recalling the way his fingertips had moved through it to cradle her skull. Her eyes went on their own volition to his hands—strong, shapely hands. Knuckles white, they lay clenched at his sides. God, can it be *that* bad kissing me? she wondered.

'You're fairly casual about where you give your

kisses. I'd have thought you could take another more or less in your stride.'

'I like to decide where I bestow them.' She was glad to see the rush of warm colour that suffused the sharp angle of his cheekbones.

'It was a mistake.' How had he done anything so stupid? he wondered angrily. 'I didn't notice you fighting me off,' he added in a goaded voice. 'Quite the contrary,' he couldn't prevent himself from concluding.

'How like a man to try and offload the blame,' Anna sneered, ignoring the accuracy of his statement. 'And I don't like being looked at like that. I'm sure you've spent years perfecting that sneer, and I can appreciate how beautifully your lip curls, but it takes more than that to impress me. As for not fighting you off, I didn't want to inflame you. Some men are turned on by that sort of thing.'

'I hope we're not going to delve into the sordid depths of your carnal knowledge. Cheap, tacky reminiscences are not really to my taste.'

Cheap…tacky! Her bosom swelled with indignation. 'At least I'm not a pretentious, self-righteous, sanctimonious bore!' she countered loudly.

'Anna!'

The sound of her name made Anna turn around to see her two sisters standing only a few feet away.

'Adam, I'm…' Rosalind came hurrying forward, closely followed by Hope.

'Don't you *dare* apologize for me,' Anna said grimly, her teeth clenched.

'Adam is our guest.'

'He's not *my* guest. I only invited people I like,' she responded childishly.

'Aunt Edie…?' Hope reminded her.

'Relations don't count. They have to come; it's Mum and Dad's ruby wedding.'

'Adam, this is Hope.' Rosalind interrupted this petty exchange with a reproving look at her sisters.

Anna watched with cynical interest as he recognised her famous sister. Hope, known as 'Lacey' professionally, had achieved fame and fortune as a supermodel. She topped Rosalind's five feet nine by two inches and was long-limbed and athletically built rather than waif-like.

Hope had the same basic ingredients as any other good-looking female, with some indefinable extra thrown in. Her mouse-brown hair had been lightened to sun-streaked glory and her lashes were dyed, but the features were the same perfect ones she'd been born with.

Men might like to drool over her on the TV screen or on glossy covers, but Anna had seen that many were intimidated when they came face to face with the real thing.

'This is a real pleasure.'

Adam Deacon wasn't one of that number, Anna noticed, seeing the look of interest in her sister's eyes as Adam clasped her outstretched hand and raised it to his lips. Anna rolled her eyes; how corny! The fact that Hope could look up into his face was in his favour: Hope was still slightly self-conscious about her height.

'Lindy tells me you're a doctor too.' The smile that launched a thousand products blazed forth. 'What have you been doing to Anna to make her lose it?' she was unable to resist asking. An impish grin replaced the sophisticated smile.

'He kissed me.'

'That was pretty daring of him.' The look Lindy exchanged with Adam was not as light-hearted as her voice; it carried a degree of censure and dismay.

'No one's told him about the left hook,' Hope added with a chuckle.

'So much for sisterly solidarity,' Anna muttered. 'As

for you, Hope, I thought you were going to spend the *entire* evening on the phone to New York.'

'Are you trying to change the subject by any chance, Anna?' Hope enquired.

'I've got things to do,' Anna said airily. She turned and walked briskly away. Her sisters were welcome to Adam Deacon.

Organising a surprise party for their parents had been a mammoth task. At least, the secret part had been in the close-knit community where everyone knew her parents. Anna had been amply rewarded for her efforts by the expression on her parents' faces when they arrived expecting a candlelit table for two and had found the whole hotel taken over for the occasion.

Anna didn't mind that they were so ecstatic to see her sisters. She was always around, but it was a treat for them to see Lindy, who was a senior house officer in a busy London hospital, and Hope, who thought nothing of visiting several countries in one week. Her visits home had been infrequent since she'd based herself in New York.

Now Anna managed to make sure everyone had a full glass to toast the couple before she joined her sisters on the podium to say a few simple words.

Charlie Lacey responded in his gruff manner, tears of emotion in his eyes and his arm around his wife.

'What can I say? Anna has kept a secret for the first time in her life!' He held his hand up and the laughter died away. 'I'm a lucky man,' he said simply, his eyes on the four women in his life.

Anna smiled insincerely as later in the evening her mother introduced her to this *nice* doctor friend of Lindy's who was going to be living locally.

'We've met,' Anna said, her dark brows meeting in a straight line over her nose.

'You've so much in common.' Beth Lacey gave a pleased smile.

'We have?' They both spoke in unison, and their eyes clashed as they each recognised the scandalised disbelief in their voices. Anna bit back the smile that quivered on her lips.

'Of course you have; you're both medical.'

'Are you a doctor too?'

'She could have been if she'd had less outside interests,' the fond mother informed him. 'She did train as a nurse, after—'

'I don't practise,' Anna interrupted smoothly. 'I found the hierarchical structure a little too confining for my taste; I branched out.'

'Into what?' Nursing must have breathed a sigh of relief to lose this anarchic spirit, he thought, watching her small hands moving expressively.

'Therapeutic massage and aromatherapy.'

'How...enterprising.'

Nasty, narrow-minded, patronising toad, she thought as she silently noted the faint, contemptuous smile. 'I take it *you're* not an advocate of alternative treatments?' She bristled with antagonism.

'Treatment—that implies that some benefit is gained?'

'I told you you had a lot in common.' Beth beamed with pleasure. 'I'll leave you children to talk shop.'

Anna noted how Adam's startled gaze followed her parent's retreat.

'No, she isn't guileless, or stupid,' she told him. Cunning would be nearer the mark, she thought affectionately. 'She keeps trying to set me up with eligible males, and I suppose she's decided you fit into that category. I've told her if she's that desperate for my room I'll move out, but nothing will do for her but to try and get me married off. It's very unfair; she doesn't interfere with Lindy and Hope, though that might have something to do with the fact they're not around.'

'You live at home?' He sounded incredulous.

'When I'm not having sex with every male in a fifty-mile radius. Mind you, I did have a wild couple of years in London before I started nursing. I didn't actually finish my training.'

'Some people find it hard to finish anything they start.'

She wasn't fooled by his neutral expression. 'We don't have your rock-solid respectability, darling,' Anna purred, aching to slap his smug, superior face.

'It wasn't a criticism, just an observation.'

'Everything you say is a criticism.' The man was aggravation incarnate!

'This is a great party. There. Is that complimentary enough for you? I believe you organised it?' At that moment a young man spun off the dance floor and hit Anna in the back, sending her straight towards Adam.

His arms opened automatically to prevent her falling. The nearly finished drink in her hand spilled down his shirt-front, and she found her cheek pressed against the damp fabric as his arms came up to steady her. A spicy, masculine aroma, the heavy thud of his heart and the tension that tautened the rock-hard muscles all made her head spin. The enforced intimacy only lasted a moment, but the light-headed sensation made her miss the cheerful enquiry from the instigator of the accident.

'It's only lemonade,' she heard herself babble, seeing the damp patch spreading across his chest. 'No permanent damage.' She lifted her eyes and met the steady, cold regard of his. 'For God's sake, I didn't do it on purpose,' she snapped, seeing the wariness in his expression. 'It wasn't a further ploy in my attempts to have your body, so you can relax.' Her breath still came in turbulent gasps as she tried to steady her racing pulses.

Adam wished he could follow her advice and relax, but tension had his spine in knots and all his anatomical knowledge wasn't going to help him unwind them. Getting the warm, womanly scent of her skin out of his nostrils might help.

'Have I done something to disturb you?' he asked, watching the colour ebb and flow in the small, vivid face of the young woman beside him. He was fascinated that anyone could have their emotions so close to the surface. Was she really as transparent as she appeared? he wondered.

'Beyond the odd grope in the undergrowth?' she asked, privately trying to analyse just what it was about this man that disturbed her so very much.

She liked open, straightforward people, and he had the sort of reticence that made a clam seem garrulous. His green eyes were secretive and mysterious and for some inexplicable reason made the pit of her stomach disintegrate. In the space where it should be was a cold and empty ache.

'I had no right to do that.' His face tightened with anger at the memory still fresh in his mind. Other parts of his body responded to the memory too!

'But you enjoyed it,' she said intuitively.

'Yes!' The stark admission seemed wrenched from him.

'If it makes it any easier,' she said huskily, 'I did too.'

His eyes gleamed momentarily with a very basic emotion. Anna watched as tiny golden lights illuminated the green darkness of the irises. The chilling expression that swiftly supplanted the warmth made her wish for once that she'd held her tongue.

'No, Anna, it doesn't make it any easier at all,' he said slowly. 'You're a wildly attractive young woman and any man would be flattered...'

But he's not, she thought, summoning a jaunty smile to cover the rising tide of humiliation that was stealing over her. She wondered whether this defence looked as pathetic as it felt.

You've really made a complete fool of yourself this time, Anna, girl, she thought angrily. The man's trying to let you down gently. She'd never laid herself so open to rejection before, and why? Just because this man had her hormones in chaos. For God's sake, Anna, she chided herself, you don't even like him.

'The thing is, I'm here to look for a house to move into with my wife...at least she will be...'

It was like being struck in the face; she actually flinched. For a moment she didn't know who she was most furious with—him for letting her glimpse a forbidden paradise, or herself for ignoring all the signals. Worse than acne or halitosis, he had a wife! I asked for this, she realised bleakly.

'Say no more,' she said in a cold little voice quite unlike the husky animation of her usual tones. She gave a light shrug as though she didn't feel as if she'd been kicked in the guts. Where was her sense of proportion? This man was a total stranger.

'I'm not nearly discreet enough for married men.' Again the light, brittle laugh. 'I can introduce you to an estate agent if you're interested; there are at least two here. Let me go find them.' Without looking at him, she moved purposefully away.

The problem with being open, she acknowledged, swallowing inexplicable tears, was you laid yourself open to a heavy share of hurt and humiliation. Her eternally optimistic heart told her one day she'd find something, or someone, worth the risk.

When one of the local estate agents she'd pointed in Adam's direction sought her out to thank her later she found even her optimism wilting.

'I might just get rid of the Old Rectory, Anna,' he observed, rubbing his hands together. 'Places that size and in that price range can be the very devil to shift.'

'Isn't that a bit big?' she said, thinking wistfully of the large Georgian house she'd always loved. It had stood empty for over a year now in the static property market.

'Not for a family of four—or was it five? Anyway he wants lots of space.'

Anna watched him move away happily visualising his sale. The lick of pure rage that swept through her made her body grow rigid and her fine eyes sparkle with wrath and contempt. What an unscrupulous, faithless, pathetic excuse of a man. She hoped she would never come across Adam Deacon again because she knew she would not be able to be civil. Married men who kissed anyone but their wives were beneath contempt as far as she was concerned.

So much for instinct, she thought in disgust—lust was all I was responding to, and I bet he was lapping up every second of it. I'm as bad as him—the creep!

CHAPTER TWO

THE rain had been falling steadily from the leaden grey skies all morning. The small group of protesters had gradually drifted away until only Anna and an elderly couple remained. Anna's arms were aching from carrying her placard, and, looking at the faces of the retired couple, she could see that they were feeling the strain.

'Shall we call it a day?' she suggested to the remaining stalwarts.

'We're fine,' the white-haired woman assured her staunchly.

'I appreciate your enthusiasm, Ruth,' Anna said with a smile. 'But there's not much point in maintaining a high public profile with no one to see us. Nobody has been in or out of the building for the past hour. We'll regroup and work out a new strategy later in the week.'

Something a bit more spectacular, Anna thought stubbornly. Something to make those philistines in the planning office sit up and take notice. Tearing down a row of Georgian cottages to make a carpark and yet another supermarket was something worth fighting about. It made her blood boil just thinking about it. If you let some planners have their way unopposed we'd end up living in a concrete jungle, she fumed.

'If you think so, Anna, dear,' George Thompson said with thinly disguised relief as he wiped the water from his brow. 'I think we will go home. Can we give you a lift?' he asked, taking his wife's arm.

'No, that's all right,' Anna said stoutly as she shouldered her placard. 'I'll take the short cut across the common.' The Thompsons lived at the opposite side of the village to her parents' farm, and the exercise would help vent her frustration.

Hood pulled lower over her eyes, head bent against the rain, she trudged off across the sodden ground. She was a member of the local ramblers' association and knew all the footpaths; she had demonstrated to keep many of them open.

The route she'd chosen took her through the grounds of the Old Rectory. Anna had decided after her parents' party the previous week that it might be tactfully expedient to avoid the Old Rectory and its new occupants for the foreseeable future.

Moving cautiously along the path that skirted the eastern border of the overgrown garden, she saw to her relief no sign of habitation in the large, uncared-for Georgian façade. With its peeling window frames and walls overgrown by a vigorous ivy the place looked deserted.

She relaxed a little, but still moved furtively along the moss-covered path, taking care she didn't slip into the brook that bisected this portion of the grounds. Her encounter with Adam Deacon had shaken her stubborn optimism more than she was prepared to admit, not to mention her confidence in her judgement.

When Lindy had casually introduced—and Anna hadn't been fooled by the *casual* part—the subject of Adam's family 'responsibilities', as her sister had so quaintly termed it, Anna had played it very cool.

'The wife and family part, you mean?' she responded in an equally offhand manner.

For once Anna wasn't prepared to have her mistakes discussed by her sisters. This was one self-inflicted hurt she wanted to keep private. No wonder Lindy had been worried if she knew Adam was a married man with a family. Anna had to live with the humiliating knowledge that she'd come on to him with all the subtlety of a sledgehammer.

Adam probably imagined that she behaved like that

with every half-decent male she came across. He wasn't to know she'd never been so attracted to anyone—at least not for a very long time, she mentally corrected. She had male friends and enjoyed their company, but romance hadn't featured much in her life. In fact her existence had been blissfully free of complications.

'Got you!' The growl of triumph along with the arm that coiled around her neck made Anna shriek in shock. The sound was cut off as the arm tightened around her windpipe, and the other one around her midriff threatened to lift her off the ground. 'Don't struggle or you'll be sorry!'

She wisely ignored this sinister advice. Without waiting to hear any more threats, she brought her placard around with all her might to strike her assailant and simultaneously lost her footing. She heard her captor's grunt of pain as he fell with her down the incline and right into the stream.

Spluttering and gasping, she surfaced from the shallow water, clutching the first thing that came to hand. Her placard had been lost in the fall. She staggered to her feet as fast as her sodden clothes would permit.

Luckily her fall had been cushioned by her attacker. Lucky for me, unlucky for him, she thought when it seemed for a moment that he was unconscious. She backed away from the supine, dark-clothed figure and looked around wildly for the quickest route of escape. She froze as she saw him move, and waved the rock in her fist in what she hoped was a menacing manner.

'I warn you, I'm a black belt in karate,' she asserted, backing away.

'You! I don't believe it.' The threatening figure sat upright and Anna saw the unmistakable features of Adam Deacon, recognisable even through a film of mud. He groaned and touched the welt on the side of his cheek.

Some of the fear that had sent adrenaline surging

through her body dispersed. The adrenaline high didn't abate even though she felt weak with relief. Excitement swirled through her veins. Happily, the visions of herself as some gruesome statistic faded away. Whatever else Adam was, he didn't fit her mental criteria of mugger or rapist. Now, if you were talking faithless swine or philanderer…!

'That I'm a black belt? I did sort of stretch the truth there,' she admitted. 'It was self-defence classes.'

'Specialising in dirty tricks, no doubt. You should carry hazard lights.' He got to his feet slowly. 'At least there's nothing broken. At least not yet.' His eyes touched the rock she still held aloft. 'If you're not going to use that do you mind putting it down? You're making me nervous. I feel as though a ten-ton truck landed on me.'

With a grimace she obliged. Not that he looked nervous. He looked angry and fairly disgruntled, which, under the circumstances, was understandable, she conceded.

'Well, what do you expect if you go leaping out on people? I only weigh seven and a half stone,' she added judiciously. 'Don't be such a wimp.'

This comment seemed to rob Adam of the breath he'd just recovered. 'You were trespassing,' he said eventually as he extracted a twig from his water-darkened hair.

'I was using a legitimate right of way, and if you consult your deeds I think—no, I *know*—you'll find I'm right.'

'Are you telling me a public footpath runs through my garden?' he demanded, momentarily sidetracked.

'It's not used too frequently.' She was beginning to shiver as the cold and damp penetrated her bones. 'But I wouldn't recommend leaping on everyone using it. It isn't the way we do things in the country.'

'Yes, a *very* friendly place, the country.' His voice was heavy with sarcasm. 'I'm down here because someone's been breaking into the place, trying to strip it of every original feature. The mouldings in the drawing room are already gone and if the culprits hadn't been interrupted last night the fireplace in there would have vanished too.'

'Not the lovely sandstone one?' Anna wailed, genuinely distressed by this news.

'It seems you know the house.' His brows shot up at her look of horror. 'If you hadn't been lurking and looking so damned furtive I wouldn't have grabbed you. You looked as guilty as sin.'

She felt a guilty colour seep up her neck until her face felt aflame. He'd hit the nail directly on the head. Guilt was exactly what she had felt. Guilt at kissing a married man and imagining in the darkness of her irresponsible dreams doing a great deal more. She silently wished Adam Deacon had stayed in the city.

'Come on,' he said impatiently. 'You can't stand there dithering. Come inside and dry out.'

Not exactly gracious, but it was the best offer she had. The idea of walking the best part of a mile home frozen to the bone with her shoes and everything else squelching was not appealing. Her docile acquiescence had nothing whatever to do with her curious and unhealthy desire to prolong this encounter, she told herself.

Why did everything about this man fascinate her? she wondered angrily, following him up the steep bank. He stopped at one point and she thought he was going to offer her his hand, but instead he pushed it deep into the pocket of his saturated jacket and gave her an uncompromising view of his broad back.

He was probably embarrassed that she had been witness to the lapse in his fidelity. Perhaps I live a bit too close to him for comfort, she thought with disgust as they entered the kitchen.

'The kitchen's the only place that's warm; I slept here last night.' He nodded in the direction of a neatly folded sleeping bag on a saggy old sofa and closed the door behind them. There were no fitted units in the high-ceilinged, stone-floored room, just an old pine table and an ancient Aga which was efficiently belting out the heat.

Anna pushed back her hood with stiff, cold fingers. She touched her hair self-consciously, aware of the shifting expression in his brooding regard. She knew she must look like a skinned rabbit with her hair plastered to her skull. She was unaware of how well her fine bone structure and clear skin stood up to critical scrutiny.

'I thought you were a boy.'

'And you prefer to leap on boys? Your secret's safe with me.'

'Are you always so glib?' he enquired harshly.

She could hardly say, Only with you, could she? The man made her so bloody defensive she couldn't seem to stop herself making facile remarks.

'Thank you, I'm not hurt,' she fired back, her voice dripping with sarcasm. It wasn't the only thing dripping; a pool of water was slowly spreading around her feet.

Adam glared at her and shrugged off the waterproof he'd been wearing. Underneath he had no shirt on, just a pair of faded jeans. His bare feet were stuffed into a pair of trainers which would probably never be the same again after their immersion. Neither would she be after seeing his torso without having the opportunity to build any sort of defences, she reflected, trying unsuccessfully not to stare.

The soberly suited consultant with the aloof air of mystery was about a million miles from this rawly masculine creature whose impressive muscles glided smoothly beneath his evenly tanned golden skin. The pulse in her neck felt as if it might explode as her eyes ran covetously over the flat tautness of his belly. There was nothing bulky about the clearly defined musculature;

he was greyhound-lean and firm. She swallowed hard and dragged her eyes higher.

His own were glittering fiercely with some indefinable emotion and her breathing grew more laboured. The fierce shrill of the kettle sitting on the hob broke the spell.

'I was making a pot of tea,' he recalled tersely, 'when I saw this highly suspicious character casing the joint. What the hell were you doing if you weren't—? Ouch!' He winced as he picked up the kettle with his bare fingers, and when he swung around he caught her involuntary grin. 'If you aren't part of the gang that's been plundering this place?' He sucked his scalded thumb and glared at her as though she were responsible for that injury too.

Physician heal thyself, she thought unsympathetically. 'I was taking a short cut home.' From broad shoulders his back tapered to lean hips that couldn't fail to look spectacularly good in wet blue denim, or just about any fabric you could mention, she pondered distractedly.

'Nice weather for it,' he observed witheringly. 'Do you always venture out fully armed? Could it be there's something the estate agent didn't tell me about this peaceful, rural oasis? Do armed gangs regularly patrol this vicinity? So far I've been ripped off before I've even moved in, and mugged.'

'Mugged!' she hooted. 'Just a bit of a scratch,' she concluded dismissively, flicking a glance at the raised welt along the side of his face.

He gave an involuntary laugh. 'You really are priceless! What the hell were you lugging around if it wasn't the latest in house-breaking equipment?'

'A placard,' she said in a tone that implied anyone but the most ignorant would have realised that.

'I might have known it; you're one of those types who protest about everything!'

A truculent expression crept over her face and her chin automatically went up.

Adam gave a scornful laugh. 'All in keeping with the fringe medicine, I suppose,' he concluded, a faint sneer curling his lips. 'Do you sit in a pyramid and meditate? Or don't you venture out if Pluto isn't in the ascendant? I suppose you think anything modern is automatically bad?'

'It's called having a social conscience,' she spat back, infuriated by his scorn. He was so typically Establishment! 'I believe in doing something about my convictions; that doesn't make me a freak. I wouldn't expect a surgeon whose answer to everything is the knife to understand that!'

'If you had a shattered leg which would you prefer— my knife or your oils? I've always suspected professional crusaders must have a big gap in their personal lives to fill.'

'Because *we're* not prepared to let faceless bureaucrats run the world? Because *we* actually care about the future? I suppose a smug, narrow-minded, terminally selfish individual might think that—' Her impassioned outburst was cut short by a fierce bout of sneezing.

'For God's sake, woman, don't stand there preaching; you'll catch cold. Get out of those things!'

'I don't preach.' She sniffed and rubbed her already pink nose. 'And I don't like being ordered about,' she added mutinously. 'Besides, I thought a cold was a virus. I can't contract a virus from wet clothes,' she pointed out pedantically.

'You sound like a spoilt four-year-old. Do as you're told!'

'If I don't?' she asked from between gritted teeth.

'Are you always so belligerent? Just for the record, if you don't voluntarily remove those clothes I will feel impelled to do it for you.'

She gave a small, startled gasp even though she'd deliberately needled him into making the threat. She pushed aside a very vivid image of his shapely fingers moving in slow motion over her own flesh, sliding beneath her wet shirt to cup one shamelessly swollen breast in the palm of his hand, and replied derisively, 'In the interests of my health, of course.' There was a husky rasp in her voice. Adam had noted it before and he liked it.

The tingle down Anna's spine made goose bumps break out over her cold skin. She wondered with deep mortification whether he had any inkling of the sinful thoughts that kept entering her head. She'd always been quite smug about resisting temptations she knew were morally wrong. She was forced to acknowledge it could be that she'd never faced a temptation she'd actually not wanted to resist before!

'Well, it wouldn't be to satisfy my curiosity, would it? That little number you wore the other night left very little unrevealed. Personally, I find mystery a little more alluring.'

'The way I recall it my blatant flaunting didn't seem to do your ardour much harm,' she flung back, incensed by his complacent criticism.

The flare of colour across his cheekbones revealed that her comments had found their mark. 'I think I should be able to restrain my baser instincts if that's what's worrying you.' He made the prospect of him not being able to sound insultingly close to a joke. 'There's some clothes in that bag.' He indicated the open holdall on the floor. 'You should be able to find something adequate to cover the essentials while those things dry. I'll turn my back, if you're feeling modest.'

Why should the idea of me having modesty be so humorous? she thought indignantly. 'I'll use the bathroom if it's all the same to you.' Her frigidly dignified tone made him grin, and reminded her she wasn't really in any position to carry off dignity.

She rumbled through the bag, trying not to notice personal items, and selected a pale blue denim shirt that ought to make a passable dress on her. With a toss of her head she stalked from the room.

After wringing out her clothes in the bath and combing her hair with her fingers, she donned the shirt, which came down to her knees, and padded barefoot back downstairs, her feet echoing on the bare boards. She tried the water to wash off the muddy stains, but it was icy cold and faintly brown.

She was shivering when she re-entered the kitchen. Adam was sipping a cup of tea. He didn't seem to be feeling the cold but at least he had put on a shirt.

'Hang your wet stuff up there.' He indicted the old-fashioned drier suspended above the Aga. His wet jeans were already hanging there. In her absence he'd exchanged them for a drier and shabbier pair. She tried not to stare at a strategic tear in the seat of them. The effort made her cheeks pink.

Hands still full of wet clothes, she looked at the pulley system that lowered the contraption with indecision.

'Here, let me.' He took the clothes from her hands before she could object and began to arrange them on the drier, not needing to adjust the height with his advantage of at least a foot.

She tried to hide her embarrassment as he shook out the more private items of her outfit; beneath the cotton drill jeans and shirt, she'd been wearing a frivolous satiny matching set of bra and pants in pale peach.

'Very *you*.' His large hand casually stroked the scrap of fabric.

'How typical!' she said in disgust, wishing desperately her colour wouldn't rise so easily at the provocation. 'And so boringly predictable. Men are nothing but large schoolboys. The mention of knickers is enough to send them into paroxysms.'

His dark brows shot up at her heated reaction. 'I just meant your underwear reflects your personality.'

'Let me guess—tawdry.' She decided to beat him to the punchline.

'Erotic,' he contradicted her firmly. His eyes held a very definite glitter that made her knees feel odd. 'Cup of tea?'

Distracted by this casual assessment, she had trouble replying to his mundane question, so accepted a cup in silence. She winced as the liquid scalded her tongue. 'It's hot,' she gasped, sitting down on a packing case pulled up to the table as a makeshift seat. Adam was seated on its twin, his long legs stretched out before him.

'You seem pretty familiar with the layout here. You knew the way to the bathroom,' he pointed out as she looked up.

'The place has been empty for quite a while. I had a look around, perfectly legitimately, with the agent. So you can stop looking so suspicious. I've always liked the place, and the previous owners didn't mix much, so I was satisfying my curiosity.'

'Current or old boyfriend?' he enquired drily. 'Or don't you differentiate? The estate agent,' he elaborated as she looked blankly at him.

'I like to keep on good terms with all my old friends.'

'I can imagine.'

'If it brightens up your drab existence I'm glad to be of service. Personally, I don't like to live vicariously, but then *I'm* not tied down.' He seemed to need reminding that he was occasionally, she thought, glaring at his handsome face disapprovingly.

'The original free spirit.'

'I have no ties; *I'm* entitled to be free.'

'Why do I think that statement is unfinished?' he said, contemplating her with weary resignation.

'Married men who go around kissing women other

than their wives don't have much room to sound so smugly sanctimonious.'

'I'm not married.'

This outright lie made her furious. She slammed her cup down on the table, slopping the liquid over the brim.

'You expect me to believe that?' she said scornfully.

'Believe what you like. As the man said, I don't give a damn.' He clicked his fingers to emphasise the point.

'You bought this house to fill the bedrooms with all your non-existent children, I suppose?'

'There are children, but I inherited them rather than participated in their conception. And, for the record, I'm engaged, not married.'

She felt a little deflated by this information, but none-theless very righteous. 'The principle is the same,' she persisted. 'How do you inherit children?' she added, consumed by curiosity.

'My brother and his wife were killed in a climbing accident,' he supplied unemotionally.

'Sorry,' she said, giving the standard, inadequate reply. Her tender heart ached for his loss but she instinctively knew he didn't want her sympathy. Adam Deacon was one of those self-contained people who didn't want anyone's sympathy. It must be terrible to love someone like that, be married to them, she reflected. Loving was as much about giving as receiving.

'Not as much as the children are,' he said grimly.

'How many?'

'Four.'

'It must have come as quite a shock to your fiancée.' Her eyes opened wide. An instant family would be a daunting prospect for any woman.

'She wasn't my fiancée at the time. Are there any other personal details you want to know? My collar size, inside leg? Feel free, but then I'm sure you will.'

They'd got engaged after he'd inherited a family. With a speculative frown she sipped her steaming brew.

'Starting married life with four children must take a bit of adjustment.'

'Starting married life at all takes some adjustment.'

Anna stared critically at him over the rim of her cup. 'I hope you can work up more enthusiasm for your fiancée.'

'I wouldn't be taking this step if it wasn't for the children.'

This calm pragmatism went against every romantic bone in her body. 'And does the lady in question know this?'

'Jessica was happy with things as they were, as I was. She's risen to the occasion magnificently.'

'I'm glad you appreciate the sacrifice.' It occurred to her that he sounded bizarrely impersonal about the whole thing. 'Have you and...Jessica been living together for long?'

'Ever heard of tactful reticence?'

Anna crossed her shapely ankles and felt no stirrings of repentance. 'If I thought you had feelings that might be hurt I'd have been more discreet, but...' Her smile silently conveyed her confident dismissal of this theory.

'I could just wait for the local grapevine to supply all the nitty-gritty details,' she suggested, pursing her lips thoughtfully. 'It'll probably take about two weeks for details to percolate down. Admittedly accuracy is sometimes sacrificed to enthusiasm—'

'Jessica and I have never lived together. *Satisfied?*'

'*Never?*'

'We both preferred to have our own space.' His patience appeared to be wearing thin.

This Jessica might of course be a saint...but Anna was deeply suspicious of a woman who wasn't after commitment and yet was happily taking on an instant family.

She whistled softly and threw Adam a gently taunting smile. 'Well, you won't have much space now, will you? If you'd wanted to get married I'd have thought you'd have done something about it by now. How long have you been seeing one another? A year…two?'

'Three as a matter of fact. I've been a friend of the family for years.'

Anna gave a derisive squawk. 'How *passionate*; you really swept her off her feet.'

'Are you implying I've pressurised Jessica?' he began.

Good Lord, he really did have an unexpected touch of naivety! Hadn't it occurred to him that this woman had found this situation an ideal opportunity to tighten her obviously tenuous hold on her man?

It could be I'm being less than generous, she conceded guiltily, swirling the dregs of her drink around in her cup. I'm certainly not jealous, she told herself firmly. This man is a monster and any woman fool enough to marry him deserves sympathy and probably therapy too. She must be unhinged.

'I'm sure she was marvellous. She might even have suggested the solution herself.' Adam viewed Anna's innocent smile with an expression of deep suspicion. 'Personally I wouldn't be flattered if a man asked me to marry him simply to be a mother to his children.'

'I seriously doubt if you'll ever find yourself in that situation.'

'Does she know you still feel inclined to grope stray females?' Anna asked, her temper climbing to smouldering point as she swallowed his contemptuous observation.

'You remind me of a stray cat. There's something very…feline about you,' he said slowly, his eyes running over her slender form, apparently losing his thread of thought. As if suddenly aware of his abstraction, he visibly stiffened, his expression hardening into a heavy frown. 'I admit I forgot myself for a brief moment, but then I've not had long to learn how engaged people act.'

'Isn't three years long enough?' Anna failed miserably to call a halt to this stream of morbid curiosity concerning his personal life. Nothing she'd heard had given her any pleasure. It was a perversely masochistic pursuit.

'I said, Anna, that Jessica and I had had a relationship for three years. I didn't say that relationship gave either of us exclusive rights.'

'You sleep around!' she accused, for some reason feeling irrationally angry.

'I'm not promiscuous, if that's what this little outburst of moral outrage is meant to imply.'

'You didn't *mind* if she slept with other men?' Anna asked incredulously. This was an attitude she found extremely baffling. She didn't think she was unusually possessive, but exclusivity was essential in her mind to any serious relationship.

'Jessica is far too tactful ever to raise the subject, and I have never enquired.'

Anna gave a choked sound of disgust. 'Very civilised!'

'I'd have thought a free spirit like you would have appreciated such an arrangement.'

'Then you thought wrong!' she cried. 'If I found a man I loved had been unfaithful I wouldn't tactfully avoid the subject...I'd...I'd...'

Adam watched with an expression of reluctant fascination as she rose to her feet. Her fists were clenched at her sides and her vivid face was a mask of passion. Her dramatically heaving bosom was hard to ignore.

'Having seen a sample of your self-defence techniques, I can well imagine what you'd do.' He slanted her a wry look. 'I'd never have tagged you as the possessive type.'

'If I was prepared to give myself unconditionally to someone I'd expect the same in return. I hate cheats...'

'Unconditionally...?'

The husky speculation in his voice and the shrewd gleam of interest in his eyes made her sink back onto her packing case. She wished fervently that she had picked anyone but this man to make such a revealing comment to.

'Let's just say you and I have a very different attitude to love and marriage.' She tried to defuse the tension between them with a casual, dismissive tone. She didn't want to touch on subjects important to her with this man who would no doubt find her impractical dream of a marriage of minds and souls amusing. His blatantly practical reason for marrying was repellent to her.

His eyes fastened onto her restless fingers plucking at the hem of his shirt, and she forced herself to lay her hands primly in her lap.

'You think the sort of passion you appear to fantasise about would stand the test of time?' He shook his head and smiled cynically. 'Lust, whilst it can be satisfying in the short term, is not much of a basis for marriage. Respect and mutual interests are a much more solid foundation.'

'I pity Jessica if all she wants from you is respect.'

'It makes more sense than basing a lifetime commitment on a purely chemical reaction,' he responded, stung by her observation. 'I mean, look at you and me...we both wanted to rip off each other's clothes the instant we met, but I'd sooner spend my days with a tornado. You're about as peaceful as a whirling dervish.'

'At least I'm not *boring*!' she replied pointedly.

His casual comment on chemical reactions had made her colour, but she was honest enough to bite back any more scornful comments because, whilst his assessment was crude, it was also basically true.

I was going to avoid Adam like the plague, but what did I do when the opportunity presented itself? she asked herself bitterly. Did I run in the opposite direction?

No. Like some idiot with lemming tendencies she'd managed to end up scantily clad and in an intimate situation with Adam Deacon. The full danger of her present situation was suddenly very apparent. She swallowed the constriction in her throat.

'*Meaning?*' he said, with a dangerous inflection in his voice and an equally daunting smile on his lips.

'*Meaning*, you give a whole new meaning to the term "stuffed shirt",' she explained helpfully. 'How old are you? Thirty-five, six? You talk as if you've mapped your life out with all the passion of a computer program.' Her lack of sympathy shone in her eyes as she warmed to her theme.

'I'm sure your motives are well intentioned. But if your brother's children have been brought up in a normal, loving environment they're not for one minute going to be fooled by neat arrangements.' Her eyes were drawn to the childish paintings pinned against the peeling plaster. 'Did they do those?'

Adam followed the line of her gaze. 'Sam and Nathan did them,' he confirmed, his voice softening as he mentioned the children. 'They're the youngest—three.'

'Twins?'

Adam nodded. 'The colours are an improvement. Until recently,' he said bleakly, 'they used black. They still have the most terrible nightmares. As things stand my mother is taking the brunt of it.' His brooding contemplation shifted to Anna's face. 'They need stability.'

'To imagine you can create security by taking a wife and moving to the country is pathetic. It takes more than an Aga and a pine dresser to give stability,' she said earnestly. Compassion for him—them—made her chest tight with suppressed emotion. 'Marriage shouldn't be a tiresome necessity, Adam.' It was warmth, sharing, and most importantly love. It was what her parents had in abundance and it was what she wanted one day.

'Wake up to the real world, Anna. You're used to getting what you want, but it doesn't work that way. In the *real* world people compromise unless they're terminally selfish.'

'Then maybe I'm selfish because I'm not prepared to compromise. That doesn't mean I don't understand reality.' She could have told him all about dashed hopes and unfulfilled dreams. 'It's you who has a problem with that. What you're going to do isn't *real*!' she said earnestly. 'It's all a fake, a lie. You can't make a home the same way they construct a film set. Mr Consultant, in your nice designer suit, don't you ever follow your instincts?' she cried scornfully. What a waste, what an awful waste, she thought miserably. I hate waste.

'It's as well for you I don't follow my instincts,' he thundered. His eyes were smouldering and his chest rose erratically in tune with his laboured inhalations. His long, clever, sensitive fingers curled into white-knuckled fists.

'What if I'm willing to take the chance?' Where had that come from? she wondered, clamping her jaw shut over any further inflammatory gems that might escape her trembling lips. The lines of stress in his chiselled features, not to mention the sinewed tautness in his neck, all betrayed the fact that Adam was close to his limit of endurance.

'Cancel that,' she babbled, making a negative gesture with her hands. 'I didn't say it.'

'I can't oblige with selective amnesia. I heard you quite distinctly.' His voice had a strained, rasping quality. Reckless was the only word she could think of to describe the glow in his half-closed eyes as he contemplated her unblinkingly.

She gave a shaky laugh, trying unsuccessfully to read his intentions. Hadn't she moments before been accusing him of being hidebound by convention, and boring? At that precise moment he looked anything but; he looked unpredictable and dangerous.

The predatory curl of his sensual lips made her already tight stomach muscles clench painfully. She licked the outline of her dry lips and tried to hide her growing sense of nervous anticipation. She tried hopelessly to catch a glimpse of the urbanity she'd poured scorn on.

'I'm renowned for saying stupid things.'

'But you mean them,' he accused, using the same tactics she frequently employed to disarm him.

Trapped by his astute assessment, she stared back at him, feeling as helpless as a moth drawn to a flame. As soon as this hackneyed analogy entered her head she felt angry. It implied she was helpless when all she had to do was get up and walk away. Alas, communications between her limbs and her brain seemed blocked; she stayed immobile.

'Come here, Anna.' The low, husky command made the hairs on the nape of her neck stand on end.

Only a fool would respond to this imperative. Why am I doing this? she wondered as she walked steadily towards him.

Adam didn't look surprised by her meek response. His eyes flared with primitive satisfaction as they ran over the length of her slender figure. She was poised before him like a wild creature, not quite sure whether to flee or not.

He reached out his hand and touched her shoulder, allowing his fingers to follow the curve of her arm. It was a light, impersonal touch that made her tremble. He was trembling too. He registered this amazing fact subconsciously as he laid his hands on her shoulders and exerted enough pressure to bring her down onto her knees before him. Sheer, primitive lust obliterated the last vestiges of rational thought from his mind.

Slowly brushing the short, silky strands of hair from her cheek, he took her small face between his hands. For what seemed like a lifetime he looked into the vivid, finely boned face tilted up to him.

Anna concentrated on breathing; it was suddenly a laborious and difficult process. Her heart thundered against her breast so loudly, she knew he must hear it.

'What if my instinct tells me to do this...? And this...?' He punctuated his words with a series of shocking, open-mouthed kisses, slow, searching and devastating. His tongue burrowed into the warm sweetness of her mouth and a ragged groan vibrated in the depths of his chest.

'You're the most bewitching piece of perfection I've ever come across,' he rasped as her throat arched to invite the attention of his mouth. His hands supported her head, which fell back bonelessly.

The primitive sound as her hands came up flat to rest against his hard belly made her shudder. His skin's warmth, penetrating the thin fabric beneath her fingertips, brought her back to a vague and dizzying sense of reality. Hazily she opened her heavy eyes and found them instantly clashing with his.

'I can't do this,' she gasped rawly. Every nerve-ending in her body was screaming in opposition. She was drowning in the taste of him on her lips, the masculine scent of him in her nostrils, the warm touch of his firm, smooth skin under her fingers.

'Why not?' he enquired, with an edge of husky indulgence that made her want to scream.

The friction as his hands moved lower over her buttocks, lifting her firmly up until she rested between the apex of his legs, made her panic. The urgency in him, the raw want, was outside her experience. He brought her knees up until she shared the makeshift seat with him, her knees either side of his narrow hips. Her position made her intimately aware of the strength of his arousal, and a rosy blush suffused her entire body.

Why not? Why not? He could actually ask that! She gasped as his hands slid under the shirt, moving in a slow, sweeping motion over the curve of her buttocks and up the dip of her waist to slide forward and cup a breast in each hand. His thumbs sought and discovered the hardened peaks and delicately set about overriding her last shreds of sanity.

'Faithless rat!'

He didn't appear to have heard her hoarse cry. Warming to her theme, and calling on her final reserve of willpower, she repeated herself in a more forceful voice. She scrambled off his lap. 'You shouldn't have to ask why not!'

'Better a rat than a vamp who cries "hands off" at the crucial moment.' Frustration and fury replaced the blankness in his eyes, but he didn't attempt to prevent her retreat.

'Vamp!' she echoed shrilly, her body shaking in reaction to the sudden plunge she'd taken from sensual pleasure to distasteful reality. His harsh jibe was enough to remind her that she'd done the right thing, but it didn't stop her from aching.

'Dear God, you're so tied up with inhibitions I'm not surprised you can't recognise plain, undiluted honesty. Contrary to your assessment I'm not into casual sex, neither do I see any need to hide the fact I find someone attractive. I did you—I hope you noticed the past tense there...*did*! Before I found out you were a narrow-minded, two-faced hypocrite. For your information I'm not some sex-starved bimbo.'

'Let your mind drift back about twenty seconds, sweetheart,' Adam drawled. His anger had been replaced by a speculative, cold expression which she found much more worrying.

'I *despise* myself for that.' She compressed her trembling lips firmly.

'I do believe you do!' he breathed incredulously.

'I need my clothes.'

'That's not what you need.' He watched the completely unexpected sheen of tears well in her wide eyes, and felt ashamed for labouring the point.

She wanted him as much as he did her. She hadn't

tried to hide the fact whereas he had done just that. He'd convinced himself that his uncharacteristic behaviour of the previous week had been an aberration. It had taken seconds of being in Anna Lacey's company to explode that myth. She fascinated him in a way that made him forget his responsibilities and act with the sense of some adolescent in the grip of a hormonal overload.

He knew his prospective marriage was a compromise for himself and Jessica, but up until now he hadn't had any serious doubts that he could fulfil his side of the bargain. So much for the man of iron, he thought scornfully, astounded at how easily and eagerly he had forgotten his responsibilities. He was disgusted and ashamed. And Anna, reading both emotions in his eyes, felt physically sick.

'I don't need any of this, Adam.'

'Then why invite it?' he asked harshly. Recriminations seemed redundant, but he couldn't help the bitterness that slipped out.

Anna recognised that he wanted to blame her for his own behaviour and she couldn't deny she had been far from innocent. 'I can't seem to help it with you,' she admitted with a catch in her voice. Her frustration and anger at this impossible situation raced to her rescue. 'Don't think I'm happy about losing my sense of discrimination and good taste!'

Her generous lips clamped shut over her gritted teeth. He's about to marry another woman, Anna, she told herself furiously, and you keep offering yourself to him. Her bizarre and contradictory behaviour was totally inexplicable.

'I think it would be best all round if we kept out of each other's way. I'd hate to upset your neat plans.'

'There's no chance of that,' Adam observed, with what she considered a heartless grin; it was as wintry as the weather outdoors.

'I'm delighted to hear it,' she told him with deep in-

sincerity. The direction of his gaze told her a little belatedly that the shirt had come unbuttoned as far as the
indentation above her navel. She snatched the fabric together.

Adam's hand came up to run down the square angle
of his jaw. He looked furious. 'Don't act as if you're not
as much to blame for this as I am,' he said heavily.
'What is it with you? Are you so used to getting any
man you want you can't let one escape your clutches?
Is this your notion of revenge for me not being smitten
the other night?'

'How dare you?' she breathed furiously. 'Don't blame
me if you can't be faithful! I won't be the scapegoat just
because your perfect relationship is full of holes.'

'Clothes,' he said, his voice staccato and flat. 'Put
them on. I'll run you home.' His face was drawn and
tense and an erratic pulse leapt in his lean cheek.

'I'll walk,' she choked. She didn't expect him to argue
the point, and he didn't. Relief…regret…Anna wasn't
sure which loomed largest in her heart.

CHAPTER THREE

THE phone woke Anna. Anna who was never ill had caught a cold that turned inexorably into flu. She'd spent the following week confined to the house. Physically she was feeling better, but the listlessness she was experiencing was almost as debilitating as the fever had been.

'Hi, Anna?' Anna heard Rosalind's voice.

'How are you, Lindy?'

'That's what I rang to ask you.'

'I'll survive.' The pause at the other end lengthened and Anna frowned. 'Are *you* all right?'

'Have you seen Adam?' The casual tone was desperately false.

'Not if I can help it,' Anna said, her stomach churning at the mere thought of the man.

The sigh echoed down the line. 'Of course not. I just wondered whether I should... No, it was a bad idea. I'll sort things out myself. I just thought he might be able to advise. No, you're right. I can do this alone. Thanks, Anna.'

'Any time,' Anna said, totally at sea. 'Do you want to tell me what's wrong?' She'd rarely heard her calm sister sound so confused and distressed. Something was wrong, badly wrong.

'It's nothing,' Rosalind reassured her brightly. 'I'm just experiencing a few teething problems settling down with the new consultant. Nothing time won't cure. We were spoilt with Adam; he's so marvellous.' There was no mistaking the deep sincerity in her sister's husky tone. 'You've no idea how much I miss him.'

Anna gasped, her mind in a whirl. How could she

have been so blind? She wasn't the only Lacey to be smitten by Adam Deacon's charm. Lindy knew him a lot better than she did; she'd worked with him for over a year. A year of being in close proximity to Adam would have sent her crazy!

'Give my love to Mum and Dad and look after yourself. Speak to you soon.'

Shaken, Anna put the phone down. She cursed herself for being a blind fool. She'd been so busy resisting—or not—the strong sexual attraction she felt for Adam that she'd not given a moment's thought to how her sister felt about him. He had come to the party with Rosalind, hadn't he? That should have told her something.

By the time she'd knotted her old housecoat around her waist, pushed her feet into a pair of slippers and glanced at her wan reflection with distaste, she was totally convinced that her sister was hopelessly in love with Adam Deacon. The only questions that remained in her mind were if he had taken advantage of Lindy's devotion and how far the affair had gone.

Anna made herself a cup of tea and prepared to take it back upstairs with her. She was feeling just the slightest bit neglected. Whilst it had seemed legitimate to grumble about her mother's fussing, she rather missed it when left to her own devices.

Where was her mum? she wondered, still fretting over her sister's broken heart. She ought to have been back a good hour ago. The sound of her mother's voice from the sitting room made her backtrack.

'I didn't know you...' She stopped, mouth open, hand on the half-open door.

'You're awake, Anna, dear. My, you really look dreadful. Doesn't she, Adam?'

'Yes, indeed,' he said, seeing no need to soften the truth. There were dark shadows beneath her wide-spaced eyes and her cheekbones seemed more pronounced in the pallor of her small face.

Looking at the vulnerability of her naked face, he found himself experiencing a dismaying surge of protectiveness. He was asking for trouble being here, he'd known that, but he'd still come.

'That damned car of mine broke down again and Adam very kindly rescued me. Come in and say hello.'

'Can't...' Anna mumbled indistinctly. She was certain those brooding eyes were missing no awful detail of her shabby appearance. She'd planned on looking cool, confident and stunning when she next saw him. She'd been going to redeem her shattered self-respect by showing how easily she could dismiss him from her life.

She'd imagined several scenarios in which he ended up grovelling at her feet. Seeing him in the flesh made her accept that Adam wasn't a grovelling sort of man!

'I wouldn't want to expose Mr Deacon to my virulent bug.'

Actually, she decided spitefully, I'd be rather pleased if his tanned complexion wasn't glowing so disgustingly with health. Ruining my life obviously agrees with him, she thought resentfully. And not just mine; poor Lindy!

'Nonsense! You're not contagious now, just feeling sorry for yourself. I was just showing Adam the—'

Anna darted forward as she saw to her horror what lay open across her mother's knees.

'No, don't!' She saw the puzzled expression in her mother's eyes and realised how loud and vehement she'd sounded. 'I'm sure Mr Deacon doesn't want to see old scrapbooks.' She tried to moderate her tone.

Inside she was deeply agitated at the idea of Adam Deacon looking at the old pictures of herself before the knee injury had turned her life in a different direction. 'We mustn't bore him.'

'I'm not bored.' Anna shot him a murderous look.

'He didn't know about your dancing.'

'Why should he?' Anna's hand shook as she placed her cup down on the table.

She felt impatient with herself. Adam Deacon was turning her into one of those silly, fluttery creatures she despised. This wouldn't do at all! Adam Deacon was bad medicine as far as the Lacey girls were concerned, she concluded dourly. At least Hope was on the other side of the world; she at least was safe.

'You've made a pot of tea. Good. You'll have one, won't you, Adam?' Without waiting for a reply, Beth bustled off.

Aloof lack of interest and cold dismissal were reactions she'd mentally rehearsed. All her meticulous plans counted for nothing now. Finding him here so unexpectedly had chased all these set pieces from her head, especially in light of her recent realisation—poor Lindy!

Her own dishevelled appearance and the fact that he was casually flicking through her life history put Anna immediately on the offensive. She wanted to demand that he explain himself over his callous behaviour towards her sensitive sister. Wasn't one of them enough? she wondered miserably.

'What was your injury?'

'Severed tendon.' She reached out and closed the heavy book on his fingers. Adam made no comment as she snatched up the collection of newspaper cuttings and held it tightly to her chest.

'Who operated?' he persisted, not taking the hint.

'Sir James Kennedy.'

'The best.'

'Isn't that you?' she snapped sarcastically. 'Lindy seems to think so. She was only saying as much to me earlier,' she said, her voice heavy with meaning. He didn't even have the decency to look guilty!

'How is Lindy?' he asked casually.

'As if you didn't know!' she said scornfully.

'If I knew I wouldn't have asked.' His brows rose at her intensity.

'She's missing your godlike presence.'

'I can understand this antagonism you have towards medicine after your experience, but Jamie Kennedy is *the* man for knees. Wasn't the operation successful?'

'I don't have any antagonism towards medicine.' Just you, she thought furiously. 'What's this, professional interest?' She gave a brittle laugh. 'Actually from your point of view it was successful, and if I'd been almost anything but a ballet dancer it wouldn't have mattered, but…'

'Tragic. Wasn't that what the critics said? "A young and startling talent lost",' he quoted accurately from a clipping he'd just read.

'I'd reserve tragedy for death, disaster and famine,' she assured him stoically. 'In the great design of things I don't think dancing is that important. Critics are prone to exaggeration.'

'When they sang your praises?'

'I was good,' she said prosaically. 'But we'll never know how good now. Lots of people who promise talent don't deliver. It's ironic that the more finely trained your body is, the more vulnerable you are.'

'It hasn't left you bitter?' His eyes raked her face as if he couldn't credit she was as well adjusted to her personal tragedy as she appeared. The newspaper clippings hinted at a glittering future. It would take an exceptional person to come to terms with losing something you'd spent half your life aiming for.

'It *could* have,' she told him, thinking back over her formative years spent with one goal in mind. She'd had a tantalising glimpse of that goal. From solo roles she'd progressed to a senior position in a touring company, and there had been talk of a new star in the ascendant. She ignored the familiar empty feeling of loss and squared her shoulders. She could do without Adam's forays into amateur psychology.

'Are you trying to tell me you are philosophical about it? You don't feel cheated?'

He really couldn't take a hint! She shrugged her slender shoulders fractionally, looking absurdly small and fragile in the oversized robe. But she wasn't fragile. Years of discipline had made her body supple and strong; that much she hadn't lost.

'I felt my share of anger and self-pity, but that passed. I decided to get on with life. I hate wasting time. I have no intention of being one of those pathetic people who prate on about their golden years when they've still most of their life in front of them. The fact is I can never dance professionally, at least not at the level I wanted to. But it doesn't stop me enjoying music.'

'I remember.'

The reminiscent gleam in his eyes made her shift uncomfortably and clutch her mementoes tighter to her bosom. 'You didn't approve,' she reminded him stiffly.

'From a distance I enjoyed it.' The corners of his mouth lifted in a reluctant smile.

'Why from a distance?' She was excited by this confession and fascinated by the smile. For a moment she forgot he'd broken her sister's heart.

'You're too...unsettling close to.' The husky admission emerged almost against his will.

'Perhaps you need a challenge.'

She was pleased he found her unsettling. Considering the traumatic effect his intrusion into her life had had it seemed only fair he should suffer some of the discomfort.

Not that she fooled herself he was anything like as confused and miserable as she was. He had his life neatly planned out and there was no place in it for her. He'd made that *very* plain.

'What are you trying to goad me into doing?' His scornful look made her squirm. He must think she was quite shameless. She *was* quite shameless where he was concerned, it seemed.

'Just making conversation.' She produced an unpicturesque handkerchief and lifted it to her reddened nose.

'Just as well; you're not dressed for seduction.'

'Thanks a lot! I really needed reminding that I look like hell.'

'I can't fight with you when you're like this,' he commented half-regretfully. 'It feels like kicking a kitten.'

'Oh, Doctor, you're all consideration,' she purred rattily. 'I'm sure Freud would have had a field day with all your feline references, but don't worry about me. I'm quite capable of looking after myself.'

'I never doubted it.'

Beth Lacey bustled in with a good-natured smile on her face. She placed a tray with tea and scones on the coffee table. 'It's so nice for Anna to have some company. She's a very impatient patient.'

Anna simmered as Adam exchanged a sympathetic glance with her mother.

'He didn't come to see me,' she said, correcting the implication that Adam Deacon was out and about visiting the sick and distressed. A saint he was not!

'All you had to do was ask,' Adam said with another sympathetic smile.

Anna ground her teeth and glared at the back of his golden head as he turned to speak to her mother. 'If I wanted company I've plenty of *friends* I'd ask.' A flush mounted her cheeks as she realised how petulant her retort had sounded.

'Did Adam tell you about the burglars?' Beth asked. 'He caught them red-handed. A gang from out of town.' Beth gave the impression that no one local would have committed such an uncivilised act. 'Did they do that to your face?' With concern she looked at the scrape down the side of his cheek.

'No, this was a stray cat.' His eyes tauntingly flickered in Anna's direction.

His fingers touched the superficial healing scar, and a

mental image of herself tracing the angry line with her tongue popped into Anna's head. She trembled with the effort of dispelling the picture.

Beth clicked her tongue in sympathy. 'Well, I think you were very brave to tackle the thugs.'

Thugs... Anna swallowed, realising for the first time that he could easily have been hurt. The desire to protect him from injury was bewilderingly strong.

'Stupid, more like,' she retorted tartly, however. 'Wouldn't it have been more sensible to leave that sort of thing to the police rather than act like some sort of macho vigilante? *They* know what they're doing.' She turned a blind eye to her mother's glare.

'Your concern for my welfare is deeply touching.' Adam deliberately misunderstood her comment, but came ironically close to the truth. 'It would hardly be realistic to expect an overstretched police force to keep a twenty-four-hour watch on an empty house. I'm no hero, Anna.'

'How cruel of you to shatter my illusions!' she moaned with a theatrical gesture.

'Anna, if you can't be civil...' her mother began in a severe tone. 'I know something that might cheer you up,' she said, diverted from her scolding. 'You'll never guess who I met in town.'

'Mother is a terrible gossip.'

'Nonsense. I just take an interest, that's all,' Beth observed in a hurt tone. 'If you're not interested...'

Anna worked her way closer to the door and resisted the temptation to smooth down her spiky hair, all the time conscious of Adam's scrutiny.

Did he always look perfect? she thought resentfully. In casual cream trousers and a tan leather jacket he looked distractingly gorgeous.

The sound of Adam's phone made Anna jump.

'Excuse me,' he said, fishing the instrument from his pocket. 'Hello, Deacon here.'

Anna tried very hard to look as if she wasn't listening. She abandoned this pretence when, after a short pause, Adam exploded.

'He—they did *what*? Why the hell would they do that? What has being three to do with it?' Adam closed his eyes and groaned.

Anna exchanged a glance with her mother who was just as fascinated by this point as she was.

'Don't panic.' Adam covered the mouthpiece with his hand and looked from Anna to Beth and back again. 'Nathan and Sam have locked themselves in the bathroom and flooded the place.'

The expression of sheer horror in his eyes made Anna's lips twitch. Domestic crises were obviously outside Adam's experience. A small, choked sound escaped her firmly clamped lips. Adam glared at her.

'I'm glad *you* find it amusing,' he snarled sarcastically. 'Two half-hysterical children are not *my* idea of a joke.' He lifted his hand to respond to the person on the other end. 'Yes, Kate, you *did* tell me they're crying.'

'You need to get them out,' Anna volunteered helpfully.

'Thank you for that pearl of wisdom.'

Anna hoped that her mother could now see how unpleasant Adam Deacon was. She threw her parent a look, but that lady was apparently fascinated by the cover of a glossy magazine. As awful as Adam was this was an emergency and Anna was concerned about these children she'd never met.

'Can they reach the lock?'

Adam conveyed this question down the line. 'All right, Kate, there's no need to yell.' He winced and moved the instrument several inches from his ear. 'It appears the leg's come off the stool.' He spoke into the phone again. 'Tell Granny I'll pay for the Persian rug to be cleaned. I'll buy her another one!' he snapped, impatience lapping at the edge of his level tones. He turned back to Anna. 'They can't turn the taps off. The plaster is falling off the drawing-room ceiling.'

This time the look he shot Anna was one of pure appeal. Adam in charge, domineering and capable, was a dynamite package, but this hint of vulnerability wrung her heart. Adam wasn't as self-sufficient as he liked to appear.

'Tell them to pull the plug out,' she suggested practically. Simple common sense often eluded intellectuals, in her experience, and here was a perfect example.

Adam hit the heel of his palm to his forehead. 'Why didn't I think of that?' He passed the advice down the line. 'They've done it. Now we've just got to get them out— Hi, Jake, what sort of lock is it? Then you could actually unscrew the mechanism from the outside. Good man,' he said with a sigh of relief. After a pause he said, 'Tell them to calm down. How?'

'Get them involved.' Anna made the suggestion tentatively.

Adam's eyes narrowed as he regarded her. He gave a sudden decisive nod. 'Here, you tell her.' He covered the distance between them in two strides and shoved the phone into her hand. Leaning one hand against the wall, he effectively prevented her from obeying her instincts and running.

She glowered at him. How typical of the man to selfishly put her on the spot. 'Hello, I'm Anna.' Her anger faded as she heard the panic in the young voice of the girl on the other end of the line.

The youthful voice identified herself as Kate, and Anna replied sympathetically. Her soft tones eventually appeared to have a soothing effect on the overwrought girl.

'Explain to them that they'll soon be out and tell them what—Jake, is it? Yes, what Jake is doing. Do they like helping him? Good. Then let them think that's what they're doing. Improvise a bit. Let them use their toothbrushes as screwdrivers and they can help Jake. Keep talking to them. Good. I'll pass you back to your uncle.' Straightening her elbow, she thrust the instrument hard into his middle.

Adam winced and his mouth twisted in a wry grin as he acknowledged her censorious frown. 'Hi, Kate.' He nodded several times and then silently mouthed, 'Thank you,' to Anna.

The glow of pleasure was out of all proportion to the token. Trying to subdue the sudden rush of colour that ran over her pale skin, she waited for him to move. He didn't, and she fought to regain her composure. Literally pushed into a corner, she couldn't help but be aware of how disturbing his physical presence was; she was only human.

Anna lost track of the situation on the other end of the line. She was unable to concentrate on anything he said before he finally rang off. He straightened to his full height and looked into her flushed, agitated face.

'The heroine of the hour.'

Suspiciously she searched for mockery but found none. 'I have a practical turn of mind,' she said half-apologetically.

'And a soft heart,' he murmured, as if he had just made the discovery. 'Kate says thank you.'

'You'll make me blush,' she replied uncertainly.

'You already are.'

'I thought I could cope with any crisis of any description.' He gave a grimace of self-disgust. 'Some parent...'

'I think you show great potential,' Anna said with an intensity that earned her a quizzical look.

His slow, steady regard was hard to bear. When her mother spoke Anna realised she'd forgotten, in the intimacy of the moment, that they weren't alone. As well for me we're not, she thought sternly. I'm about as covert as an earthquake.

'Anna is one of those rare people who have never forgotten how it feels to be a child. That sort of empathy is rare.'

'*Anna's* rare.'

It was, she thought, almost as if Adam too had forgotten they weren't alone, from the way he looked at her. A solid lump of hot emotion welled in her throat. A wave of debilitating weakness that had nothing to do with flu swamped her.

'I'm glad things worked out,' she said, with the merest hint of a tremor in her voice. She clenched her fists whilst searching for inspiration to dispel the strange intimacy which had built up. 'Go on, Mother, you were aching to spill the dirt.'

Looking at her mother helped prevent her eyes from straying to the way Adam's blond hair curled ever so slightly against his tanned neck. Bad medicine—that was Adam Deacon!

'Simon Morgan is back!'

Anna knew she had been a caricature of startled dismay for all of twenty seconds before she managed to recover from this piece of news. She shot Adam a defensive glare and he smiled back sunnily, all white teeth and benign disinterest. It was too much to hope he hadn't noticed her monumental slip.

'That's nice,' she floundered.

'I knew you'd be pleased,' Beth continued happily. 'Anna and Simon were really close all through school,' she explained helpfully. 'I always encouraged the girls to have different friends and interests. So many people treat twins and triplets as a single entity. Simon went off to Canada about four years ago now. How time flies.'

'Is the whole family over?' Anna asked dutifully, even though it was the last subject she wanted to discuss in front of Adam. The whole family... Simon, Rachel and their baby, who probably wasn't a baby any more.

'Split up,' Beth said in a hushed tone.

Anna swallowed. Having Simon unavailable and married she could accept. Knowing the situation was different and that he was right here needed some quiet time for reflection. How did she feel about it?

'I'm a bit tired; I think I'll go back to bed,' she mumbled, regardless of the impression her hasty retreat would give.

Breathless after taking the stairs two at a time, she threw herself on her bed and inhaled deeply, staring blankly at the ceiling. After all these years Simon was back, without Rachel.

Her best friend from the age of eight, she had imagined she knew him better than anyone else. As things had turned out she couldn't have been more wrong.

She could still see his laughing face as he'd confessed ruefully to harbouring a passion for her for years. To add insult to injury he'd chosen his own wedding day to make the admission.

'Only I didn't want to ruin a beautiful friendship, Anna. You were obviously not interested. It seems ridiculous now. I always knew you didn't have much time for relationships with your dedication to dancing,' he'd told her.

The irony of the situation had made her unable to reply without making a total fool of herself. She'd been crazy about him for years! She had vowed at that moment never again to waste an opportunity for happiness by hiding her feelings. Life was filled with 'if only's. But sometimes she wondered... Now he was back—and alone!

CHAPTER FOUR

'WHAT are you doing here?' Anna swung upright, hugging her knees to her chest as she registered a hostile presence in her sanctuary.

'Your mother sent me with your tea; you forgot it.' Adam calmly placed the cup on her bedside table and looked around with interest.

'Don't let me detain you.'

'Not very tidy, are you?' He picked up a delicate bra from the floor and swung it around on his finger.

'Give that here,' she snapped, grabbing for it.

Adam took a step back, holding the scrap of peach satin just out of her reach. 'Please.'

'Go to hell!'

'So unladylike,' he murmured regretfully.

'What do you think…?' she began furiously as he sat down on the side of her bed.

The cheek of the man! She stifled a flurry of alarm as the bed creaked under his weight. Her bed and his weight linked themselves in her subconscious and gave birth to a whole series of connected images that she fiercely hoped weren't reflected in her expression. Beads of perspiration broke out over her upper lip and she dabbed them gently with the tip of her tongue.

'Tell me about Simon,' Adam said abruptly, annoyed to find his attention riveted to the pink tip of her tongue. He couldn't explain the animosity he felt towards this faceless person. This young woman's lovers were nothing to him.

'There's nothing to tell,' she said coldly. 'Lurid' hardly described the pictures in her head!

'Sure,' he drawled, his face harshly sceptical. 'You should have seen your face back there.' His expression grew sourly cynical. 'Did he dump you? Or don't you have staying power?'

'For your information Simon and I were just...'

'Good friends?' he completed for her with a sneer. 'No one looks like *that* hearing a "good friend" is back in the country. If you gave off the same signals back then as you do now he must have been extraordinarily dense if that is true.'

'Simon is not dense!' she responded, angry at his disparaging air.

The thin smile was sly and calculating. 'Just available,' he observed silkily, watching her from beneath his heavy eyelids.

Lashes as long and thick as her own cast a faint shadow across the curve of his cheekbones. He gained little comfort from her guilty flush at this jibe. Why the hell couldn't he leave well alone and keep away from Anna Lacey? he asked himself angrily. He had no right to be thinking about her. Let her make it up with her old flame.

Anna watched Adam as he looked, grim-faced, around her feminine room with its clutter, some of it left over from her teens. She felt as if signs of her immaturity were all around them. How was he squaring his opinion of her with the teddy bear minus an ear? She could suddenly sympathise with people who suffered from claustrophobia. Having Adam in the confines of her bedroom was making her feel trapped and panicky.

'I'm sorry if he's having marital difficulties, but I'm sure they'll be resolved.'

I'm not the sort of person who'd want happiness from others' misery, she thought, resenting his implication. Unless that misery is Adam Deacon's, a nasty, spiteful voice in her head added. One minute she felt fiercely protective of him, the next she felt spitefully vicious. It left her in a constant state of confusion.

When Adam ran a finger along the delicate arch of her foot she bit back a yelp and retracted it. 'How self-less of you.'

'I don't know where you get off questioning me about my affairs,' she said, glaring at him furiously.

'I thought we were talking pure friendship, untainted by the spectre of sex, here.'

'Don't be childish!'

'That would never do, would it?' he mocked, picking up a threadbare rag doll from the foot of the bed. 'I'm only returning the compliment, you know—you were so *very* interested in my personal life, it only seems polite to show some interest in yours. I have to admit I thought you'd be silk sheets and see-through lingerie, not patchwork and winceyette.' He gave a low chuckle.

'It's cotton,' she retorted, her pride stung by his amusement. As much as it angered her to be thought of as some oversexed vamp she found she preferred it to being stigmatised as a frump.

Taking the comment as an invitation, he reached out and pulled the tie on her dressing gown, and proceeded to take the fabric of her nightdress between his thumb and forefinger. His knuckle moved against her collarbone as he rubbed the material. The buzzing in her ears became a loud hum as his eyes captured her own fluttering gaze.

'How is Jessica?' Instinctively she used the key to break the spell. Ruthless reality did it every time. She almost whimpered with relief—or was it regret—when he straightened up.

'She's coming up to see the house tonight.' The timely reminder made his expression grow cold and shuttered.

'Meaning she hasn't yet?'

'She trusts my judgement.' He frowned at her critical tone.

In truth he wasn't entirely sure about what Jessica's response to the Old Rectory would be. It didn't fit the criteria for a home they had both so painstakingly agreed on, but somehow the place had seemed *right* the moment he'd seen it. He wasn't prone to making emotional decisions based on gut reaction, and it intermittently bothered him that he'd done so over such an important matter.

'Sounds pretty wet to me,' she observed with disgust.

'We want the same things.' Hearing the betraying defensive note in his own voice brought a self-derisive twist to his lips.

'How sweet,' she trilled mockingly.

'Spite, Anna?'

'Go away; I'm ill,' she mumbled, turning her head and pushing it into the pillow.

She felt ashamed of her acid retort, but wasn't about to let him see her contrition. The pillow was suddenly yanked out from beneath her head. She sat up indignantly to see Adam standing holding it beside her.

'Don't worry, I won't tell her that her future husband is a lecher.'

'Your concern is misplaced; Jessica doesn't get upset about insignificant details. After all, what are a few kisses,' he said dismissively, 'when compared with what Jessica and I have?'

'Insignif...?' She inhaled as wrath widened her eyes. She picked up a pillow and swung it in a wild arc, hitting him directly in the midriff. That'll wipe the supercilious smirk off his face, she thought. He grunted with surprise at the impact; she'd put all her wiry strength behind the blow.

'Ouch!' she yelped as he retaliated in kind, swinging the pillow he still held at her. 'You bully!' she cried indignantly, scrambling to her feet on top of the bed.

This time she aimed for his head, but he neatly ducked and simultaneously scooped her in a fireman's lift over his shoulder. Letting go of the pillow, she hammered her fists against his back and swung her feet in an equally vicious assault on his front. 'Let me go!' she gasped furiously.

Adam was breathing heavily; he swore and pushed aside the loose folds of her dressing gown which were effectively blinding him. The blows Anna was landing were by no means innocuous. He tipped her unceremoniously onto her back on the bed and came to rest above her on his knees, with his hands at either side of her head.

The anger slowly faded from her face as she found herself staring up at him. Beneath the anger there was a fierce, raw expression; it was riveting. A slow, seductive lethargy seeped insidiously through her veins. Nervously, her breath coming in short gasps that had little to do with the recent exertion, she licked her dry lips. Adam's eyes faithfully followed the action. Anna could see the light burning under the heavy droop of his eyelids.

'How did we get here?' he asked in a hoarse voice, as if he'd lost track of the events that had brought them to this position. He hadn't moved since the moment their eyes had collided, but his gaze moved continually over her supine form.

'You called me in...insignificant.'

His voice held a bitter edge of irony. 'Well, that was a lie, wasn't it? Insignificant is the last thing anyone could call you.' One of his hands moved to gently skim the side of her face. 'If the circumstances were different...' Frustration was evident in his deep voice. He moved his fingers clear of her skin, but they flexed as if they wanted to return.

'Different?' she echoed, feeling as strange as this conversation.

'But they're not!' The high, sharp lines of his cheek-bones seemed more prominent as his expression taut-ened. Denial warred with want in his eyes, and no victor emerged. 'I have responsibilities, commitments; I can't permit myself...

'It's wrong of me to blame you.' She was literally shaking under the onslaught of deep, primitive need. 'You can't help being who you are, what you are... You go through life reacting to stimuli without any thought of the consequences.'

His words stunned her. Her heart was thudding so hard she could hardly breathe. 'What am I?' Other than totally unfitted to having a relationship with such an el-evated personage as Adam Deacon, she added silently.

'You're unorthodox, spontaneous, erratic and...' she could see the muscles in his throat working... 'sinfully sensual.'

'And that's bad?' She reached up and pushed her fin-gers into his hair until her fingertips met at the back of his neck. 'I've wanted to do that for ever,' she admitted, indulging in some dangerous honesty of her own. Hon-esty was a luxury these days.

If this was what 'reacting to stimuli' felt like, she could recommend it. She felt the muscles in his neck bunch beneath her fingers. She wasn't being fair, but then, she thought with a sudden flurry of anger, neither was he.

'You're an adventure I'd have welcomed before,' he said hoarsely, allowing her hands to draw him lower. His lips nuzzled the soft flesh at the side of her mouth.

Anna gasped silently as rivulets of sensation followed the sensual stroke of his tongue. She recognised the warm, musky scent of his skin and stared with fascina-tion at the gold flecks in his marvellous eyes.

'Before you lost your sense of adventure?' she whis-pered back. She was having trouble forming words by this point. Every fibre of her being was screaming out for attention from that stern, yet incredibly sensitive mouth.

'I have a family now.' The strain cracked his voice, and he allowed his head to come to rest against her chest. 'I owe it to them. Stability...' he added almost vaguely. He lifted his head and seemed unable to tear his eyes away from the physical evidence of the tingling she could feel in her breasts.

'Jessica.' She made a last-ditch attempt to do the right thing. Part of her hoped it would work, but the other part...!

'They need a mother, a stable influence. Ben and Tess were fantastic parents.'

'I've heard a lot about what they need. What do *you* need?' she persisted. Her soft brown eyes, fierce and hugely dilated, were fixed with reproachful anger on his face.

'This sort of passion burns itself out as quickly as it...' He spoke as if he was trying to convince himself as much as her.

He let out a groan as she ran a questing hand over the taut muscles in his thigh. He caught it and redirected it until she couldn't mistake his needs.

'I need you! Is that what you want to hear?' he demanded bitterly as he thrust her hand away. 'Well, I do, as badly as some adolescent in the first throes of infatuation. No fool like an old fool, is there?'

'You're not old.' The undertone of anger and resentment in his voice sobered Anna. No wonder he thought her a wanton baggage; she hardly recognised herself these days.

She hadn't been shocked by the intimacy of moments before, but she had been excited in a dry-throated, heart-pounding, reckless sort of way. It might have been easier to come to terms with indifference! she thought despairingly.

'When I look at you I feel it.'

'You're so stupid!' she wailed angrily. He spoke as if the foundations of his future were set in cement. He obviously didn't love that dratted woman—this situation couldn't exist if he did.

If he loved Jessica, Anna reasoned, he wouldn't want me. To marry to fulfil some ridiculous idea he had of a perfect nuclear family was a recipe for disaster. What did it matter to her if the man ruined his life? she asked herself angrily. And why did he have to slot her into some wretched category? she wondered. What heading was she filed under? Instability and possible moral degeneration? The possibility that they could have anything more in common than mutual attraction had obviously never occurred to him. I'm the sort of woman children should be protected from, she thought, repressing a bubble of semi-hysterical laughter.

Why should I care? Let him ruin his life. Like a bolt of lightning the answer popped into her mind. She shook her head in mute denial. She couldn't love him; she didn't even like him!

Adam's hand slid beneath her skull and he kissed her hard on the lips. She could feel the desperation in him right through to her bones.

'Stupid doesn't begin to cover it,' he said huskily as he lifted his head. 'I didn't have to come up here. Your mother didn't suggest anything; I did. I wanted to prove I could be alone with you and not...not do this.' His voice was slurred as he ran his hand down the length of her slender body from shoulder to flank. 'Or maybe that I could do this and then stop.'

Anna was frightened by the oddly unfocused expression in his absinthe eyes as he stared down at her.

'Enough, Adam!' she said in a hoarse voice. One of them had to call a halt to this situation, and he didn't look as if he could.

'I want you.'

'That's not enough, not nearly enough,' she told him, hoping she sounded firmer about this than she felt.

Adam closed his eyes and muttered something from between compressed lips. After a few moments he seemed to regain some degree of control. He moved, but only to roll on his side beside her. He raked his fingers through his blond mop of hair. She'd dreamt about his head occupying the pillow beside her, but now it was happening she couldn't look at him.

'What are you saying?' he demanded flatly.

'I'm saying wanting me isn't enough. I'm not into empty sexual experiences, and you're not into one-night stands. Wasn't that what you told me?'

She heard the sharp inhalation as he caught his breath, and allowed her head to turn when he captured her chin between his thumb and forefinger. She met his turbulent gaze with all the calm she could muster, even though her nerves were breaking new records for endurance.

'Great!' she said bitterly. 'It's fine for *you* to look insulted now, but *I'm* not supposed to care if all you want from me is a quick tumble. I've heard all about *your* suffering as you try and control these primal lusts,' she drawled sarcastically. 'But not once have you asked me how *I* feel.

'Do you think I'm flattered? Just because you've decided to put your principles on hold for the duration, what makes you think I'm happy to do the same?' She gave an angry snort at the look of disdain that flickered across his handsome features. 'Just because I'm not as narrow-minded or as conventional as you doesn't mean I don't have a sense of morality.'

'I'm not talking philosophy, Anna. It's more relevant that I *know* how you feel every time I touch you! I don't need to ask you,' he retorted confidently, his colour heightened. 'Or are you now going to tell me this is all one-sided?'

'I'm trying to tell you I don't indulge in shallow,

superficial affairs which might be satisfying at the time, but leave a nasty taste in the mouth. Neither do I sleep with married or engaged men.'

'When did you formulate this worthy philosophy?' he demanded contemptuously. 'In the last sixty seconds? Isn't it a bit late to be setting arbitrary rules? Do you get some sort of kick out of pushing men to the limit? It's a dangerous game, Anna,' he warned grimly.

'I'm only telling you the truth,' she said unhappily. 'Did I engineer any of our encounters? They've just happened. I can't change the way I feel about things just because you make me feel...' She stopped, biting her full lower lip in anguish.

'How do I make you feel?' he demanded, his fingers tightening painfully around her jaw.

She shook her head, refusing to answer that one. 'When I share my body I want it to be with someone who is interested in *me*—not someone who is opposed on principle to everything I believe in. You see, basically we're in agreement that it takes more than a chemical reaction to make a relationship, Adam. You may be prepared to settle for something less, but I'm not!'

Both were so involved with one another that they didn't hear Beth until she was halfway into the room. She took one look at the pair on the bed and her eyes widened.

'So sorry, Simon, we'd better make it tomorrow,' she said in a loud voice, and backed swiftly from the room. 'She's still busy with the doctor,' Anna heard her say in the hallway.

'I've never been so humiliated in my life!' Anna groaned, sliding off the opposite side of the bed.

'"She's still busy with the doctor,"' Adam repeated, sitting up. The sound of his ironic laughter rang out. 'That sort of bedside manner could get a man in trouble. She really does have a nice sense of irony, your mother.'

Anna stopped wringing her hands and glared at him

with distaste. 'I'm so glad *you* find it amusing,' she spat furiously. 'Stop laughing,' she added urgently. 'What will Simon think?'

Adam's face abruptly hardened, and she hated the silky sound of his voice when he spoke. 'Simon—of course. Is that why you've suddenly come over with a case of morality? I take it a married man who's separated from his wife doesn't enter the restricted zone?'

Anna picked an amber-headed hat pin from the red heart-shaped pin-cushion that housed part of her collection of decorative pins. She looked pointedly at the tip and then at Adam.

'If you don't want to have more than a scratched face to explain to your lady love, I'd make tracks,' she said with soft fury. How typical that male vanity had to rationalise rejection, she thought darkly, stabbing the point back home into the velvet.

'My God, you may have lost your ability to dance, but you sure as hell kept your artistic temperament intact.' He saw her flinch and her slender back visibly stiffen. 'That was uncalled for.' The flicker of distaste that crossed his face was not aimed at her.

'It's nothing less than what I've come to expect of you in the short time I've known you.'

'I'm not usually such a brute.'

'I feel uniquely privileged,' she snapped sarcastically.

'I've tried ignoring the way you make me feel...'

'And what way is that?'

'Hungry.'

The single word was raw and needy. She shuddered under the impact of his hot, fixed stare which was filled with as much resentment as desire.

'The solution is obvious,' Adam continued.

She had to hear this one. 'Would you like to share it?'

'If we feed the hunger it should vanish as swiftly as it occurred.'

'Let me get this straight,' she said, forming the words with care. 'I should sleep with you so that you can marry Jessica and be the perfect father figure, with this temporary insanity put firmly behind you.'

'I wouldn't have phrased it quite like that...'

'I just bet you wouldn't!' He really is serious! she thought incredulously.

'You're the one who prides herself on a straightforward approach. A lot of men would have taken what you were offering and run. I've tried to be straight with you. Be realistic, Anna.'

'You're mad!' The casual way he insulted her defied belief.

'Believe me, it doesn't give me any pleasure to admit to this weakness,' he said harshly. 'In fact I wish I'd never set eyes on you!'

'And the maiden, overcome by his romantic declaration, fell into a swoon,' she trilled angrily. 'You have a novel way of propositioning a girl, Adam. Ten out of ten for originality.'

'I suppose you'd prefer me to be mawkishly sentimental?' he suggested, his eyebrows lifting as if he was mildly surprised by her reaction.

'Heaven forbid,' she choked. 'You're the most arrogant, insensitive man I've ever met!' she breathed furiously.

'I don't much like you either, but we're not talking about our undeniable incompatibility here. The common denominator which draws us together appears to be lust, pure and simple, and you're fooling yourself if you think you can hold out against it.'

'You think you're that irresistible?' she jeered.

'No, you are!'

Anna was still recovering from his parting shot when her mother returned. Beth replaced the cold cup of tea with a steaming one, and regarded her daughter quizzically.

'I suppose you're shocked.'

'Shocked?'

'I was kissing a man engaged to someone else.' I deserve to be despised, she thought dolefully.

'Well, I didn't see that part, but I did assume.'

'It was my fault,' Anna confessed miserably.

'Not according to Adam. He said you were entirely blameless.'

Anna's eyes opened wide. 'He said *what*?'

'He said you were a blameless victim, or words to that effect, when he was apologizing for abusing my hospitality.'

'I don't believe it... What did you say?' The man was a constant source of surprise to her. Old-fashioned chivalry and lethal lust made an uneasy combination, and a painful one, she suspected.

'I assured him that my Anna didn't know how to be a victim, and that as much as I would like to protect all my daughters you were past the age where that was possible or practicable. I did make it pretty clear that we take a dim view of anyone who hurts our girls.'

'Oh, Mum,' Anna breathed, tears shining in her eyes. 'I don't know what I'd do without you.' She buried her face against a motherly bosom as she choked back a sob.

'I also told him that you were capable of deciding who you wanted to kiss. We always let you take your friends up to your rooms when you were teenagers; I can hardly start laying down the law now.'

'You always were a liberal parent,' Anna responded with a watery smile. 'I don't think Adam is as open-minded as you. Wanting me is tearing him to bits. He'll end up hating me, if he doesn't already.'

'And what is it doing to you, darling?'

Anna shook her head mutely. Her own feelings were too confused to share with anyone just now—even her mother. She knew just how lucky she was to have her parents there when she needed them.

'I do trust your judgement, Anna.'

Anna lifted her head, and tears were streaming down her cheeks. 'I'm not sure I do,' she said simply.

CHAPTER FIVE

ADAM turned the corner and found himself at the end of a long queue of cars. 'This is the sort of thing I was supposed to have left behind in the city.' He glanced impatiently at his wristwatch.

Jessica laid a pacific red-nailed hand on his arm and smiled sympathetically. 'Poor darling.'

A relationship which up until recently had consisted of civilised excursions to the theatre and restaurants followed by intimate evenings alone meant Jessica had never experienced the more difficult side of Adam's nature. She carefully kept her displeasure to herself.

The teenaged girl in the back of the Range Rover saw the possessive gesture and grimaced at her elder brother. Jake, aware that his uncle was watching them through the rear-view mirror, shot her a warning glance. On balance they'd decided that subtlety might be a better bet than outright hostility to get rid of the ghastly Jessie. The little ones were too young to be of any use, but Jake and Kate were determined to throw a few spanners in the works.

'I need to go!' a small but determined voice announced.

'You only went just before we left the house,' Kate observed, frowning at the youngest of her siblings.

'I want to go too,' an identical voice announced sleepily.

Kate and Jake glanced at the mutinous expressions on their three-year-old twin brothers' faces and said in unison, 'They need to go, Uncle Adam!'

'What am I supposed to do about it?' Adam appealed

for guidance as a large van pulled up behind them, effectively blocking them in.

'I don't know,' Jake said cheerfully. 'But sooner might be better than later,' he added as his brothers both began squirming in their seats.

'They'll have to wait,' Jessica announced, as though that put an end to the matter. 'Are those television cameras?' Her attention was diverted as a group of people lugging equipment jumped from the van behind them and headed off in the direction of the town. She glanced at her reflection in the mirror with a thoughtful expression. 'Perhaps we should go and find them a lavatory, darling,' she suggested.

'Good idea, Jessie,' Jake said as she examined her perfectly applied lipstick in the mirror.

'Jessica,' Adam corrected grimly as his fiancée shuddered at the detested diminutive. The constant sniping was trying his patience.

'It just slipped out,' Jake said apologetically.

'Don't let it slip again,' came the dry advice. 'There's no need for everyone to come,' he added as all the occupants of the vehicle followed him out of the car.

'We're not coming to help you,' Kate said. 'We want to find out why the cameras are here. Like everyone else,' she added as the occupants of most of the cars trapped in the jam made their way along the road.

'Children are so curious.' Jessica smiled tolerantly. She couldn't resist a last glance at her reflection in the wing mirror.

'Jess…Jessica can look after the boys as she's not interested,' Kate observed helpfully. She placed one of her brother's hot and grubby paws firmly in the tall blonde's manicured hand. 'Don't worry, it's only chocolate,' she said sweetly as Jessica examined with ill-concealed horror the dark stain on her pale linen skirt. 'Nothing toxic.'

'Sam doesn't want to go with *her*,' the twin with his hand in Adam's announced.

'No, I don't,' his more placid twin agreed readily. Jessica gave a brave smile, but didn't resist when the boy twisted his fingers from her own.

'Poor little things. All this trauma is bound to have an impact, but I do think it's a mistake to let discipline suffer.' The tinge of martyrdom in her smile was nicely judged.

Adam's expression remained impassive as he turned and caught his niece doing a passable mime of gagging behind his fiancée's back. He kept silent on the subject of discipline. 'Let's get this circus on the road,' he said briskly, taking a twin in each hand and heaving them up into his arms.

About two hundred yards down the road it became clear that more than one camera crew was present. It seemed a safe bet that the fifty or so protesters clad in Regency dress and wielding large placards might have something to do with this fact.

The whole town square had been turned into a scene from Jane Austen, and the crowd of onlookers watched in bemused fascination as ladies in pastel-coloured, high-waisted dresses wafted past beside men in skin-tight pantaloons and high collars.

'Bringing the town to a standstill on market day is typical of the selfish behaviour of this bizarre group who are opposed, on principle, to progress. What about the jobs? What about the…?' A large man whose grey suit didn't quite cover his spreading middle and also proclaimed he had nothing to do with the demonstrators spoke into the microphone with an air of authority.

A small figure stepped forward from the other side of the young man holding the microphone. 'We don't need another supermarket. We don't need a carpark. Those cottages are a legacy,' she said earnestly, looking into the camera.

The breeze blew the folds of her lavender muslin gown against her legs, and she held tightly onto her swansdown-trimmed bonnet. Her bosom heaved effectively in the low-cut gown, a fact that kept drawing the cameraman's attention.

If she lost any of the costumes the local amateur dramatic society had lent them from their forthcoming production of *She Stoops to Conquer* Anna knew she would be dead meat.

'If they were listed...'

'Mr Shaw is aware that we are in the process of applying for historical listing.'

'We're not talking Bath's grand parade here, just a sad group of neglected tithe cottages.' He gave a disdainful laugh, and Anna resisted the strong impulse to kick his shins. She had a much better way to take that condescending smirk off his face.

'Tell me, Mr Shaw, am I right when I say you have a close personal interest in this supermarket going ahead?'

'I'm interested in the good of this town, young lady, which is more than you and your group of crackpots are.'

'I ask,' Anna continued in a clear voice that could be heard across the square, 'because I have learnt that the successful building contractor for the scheme is your son-in-law.'

'My son-in-law isn't a builder.' The reply was firm enough, but the man's pale eyes held the first signs of caution.

'And you would have declared any conflicting interest you had, I'm sure. Your son-in-law *is* an executive director of the building firm which has won the very lucrative contract for the supermarket development. You and he have several joint financial ventures, I understand...'

Anna stepped back happily. The reporter had enough

Rottweiler in him to scent blood. She heaved her banner onto her shoulder and joined the chanting group that was blocking the highway.

Something made her look to her right; on the perimeter of the crowd her eyes paused and stopped. Tall and blond-headed, the man stood out from this crowd as he would from any. He held two angelic-looking boys and he was staring straight at her. Their eyes met, and her heart seemed to stop. Her stomach muscles contracted painfully and all the strength rushed from her limbs, leaving her feeling strangely empty.

The smile faded dramatically from her face and it took her several moments to tear her eyes away. She responded to an anxious enquiry at her side with a firm nod.

'I'm fine,' she lied.

'You looked so odd just then. I thought you were going to pass out,' Ruth Thompson confided.

'I was nervous with the cameras,' Anna improvised, keeping her profile firmly averted from a certain tall figure. In truth she would have preferred to face a thousand cameras than Adam Deacon. Was it always going to be like this? she wondered bleakly.

'Well, it didn't show, you were so natural. I think the period costumes were a brilliant idea, and who'd have thought all these TV people would turn up?'

Anna's smile held a hint of irony. After the hours she'd spent ringing around to ensure the press coverage today she would have been devastated if they hadn't turned up.

'It looks like Mr Shaw has had enough.' Anna watched as the big man shouldered his way past the media and got into his official chauffeur-driven limousine.

The driver inched his way forward, his hand on the horn. People leapt hastily to one side as the vehicle gath-

ered momentum. It all happened so quickly that Anna
couldn't recall the precise sequence of events afterwards.

It looked as though Ruth had plenty of time to move
aside, but Anna knew that the elderly woman's arthritic
hip made her slow. She shot forward, a cry of warning
on her lips. Somehow she was between the car and the
grey-haired figure, and the next thing she was thrust vio-
lently forward. Her hands saved her face from the tar-
macked surface, but her knees took most of the impact.

There was a lot of noise and loud jeers as the car came
to a halt. She ignored the anxious voices of concern all
around her; all she could think about was the hole she'd
torn in the costume she'd promised to return in pristine
condition.

'Fine…I'm fine,' she said vaguely, shrugging away
the hands that were extended to help her up. The pain
in her knee when she shifted her weight took her breath
away. No, not again, she found herself silently praying.

'She saved my life,' a tremulous voice announced
somewhere to Anna's left, and then she heard Simon's
familiar tones beside her.

'Are you hurt?'

'It's my knee,' she hissed.

'Here, let me…'

'No!' Panic seized her as he took hold of her shoulder.
'Simon, I can't move, it'll…' She gritted her teeth as
her throat dried up.

'Love, you can't stay like that,' Simon said reasonably.

'I'm a doctor—can you give us some space, please?'
The answer to Simon's prayers pushed him unceremoniously to one side.

Adam *would* feel morally obliged to step forward,
Anna thought, biting her lip. She could just imagine how
much her actions had confirmed his opinion of her reckless immaturity.

'Go away, Adam!' she pleaded from between compressed lips. She sensed him kneel beside her and stayed crouched on all fours, her eyes tightly shut.

'I've never seen anything so wantonly stupid.' His low, furious voice gave her no desire to open her eyes.

'I think she was very brave,' a young male voice she didn't recognise said admiringly. 'And fast.'

'The last thing she needs is encouragement,' Adam retorted grimly. 'Can you move?' he asked, his voice growing more impersonal. She felt his hands on the back of her neck.

'Do you think I'm on my hands and knees because I like it?' The snarling sarcasm ended with more of a whimper than a roar, and she felt the prick of tears behind her eyelids. 'I think I've hurt my knee—the bad one. It hurts like blazes.'

'I hardly think yelling at her is going to help.' Simon's indignant expression made it clear he didn't think much of the older man's bedside manner.

Adam turned to look at the owner of the critical voice. He saw a pleasant-looking young man, of above average height, clothed in period dress, who laid a protective hand on Anna's shoulder as he went down on one knee.

'For God's sake, Simon, don't get a mark on those pantaloons. I've already ruined one outfit.' Anna betrayed little gratitude at his intervention. She squinted sideways and moaned as he placed the other yellow-clad knee on the dusty ground.

'See?' Simon said anxiously. 'She's in pain!'

'Thank you for your valuable input.' Anna inwardly winced at the sarcasm in Adam's voice. 'If you move to one side I might be able to make my own diagnosis.'

'We've only your word for it you are a doctor,' Simon said, his colour heightened with anger.

'Not a doctor!' Jessica intervened indignantly. 'I'll have you know he was one of the youngest professors in the history of the hospital. Adam, I really don't think you should get involved with these people. You hear all sorts of stories about doctors being sued for malpractice after roadside heroics. You should consider your best interests, darling. I'm sure an ambulance will be along soon; they're much better equipped to help.'

'It's my patient's best interests I'm concerned about, Jessica! Do something useful—look after the twins. Get that bloody camera out of my face,' he added softly, with a savage smile that made the news-hungry media hound step backwards.

Adam's fiancée paled at this sharp reprimand. 'I was only offering my advice.' Her public-relations soul was clearly shocked by anyone speaking to the media so bluntly. 'He didn't mean it,' she apologised hastily to the reporter.

'Anna, I'm going to get you off that knee.' Adam's attention was totally on the injured girl as he ignored the circus surrounding them.

'I'm scared to move,' she admitted gruffly, rather ashamed of this cowardly behaviour. Memories of how badly her knee had hurt the first time held her frozen and made her limbs shake. He must think I'm pathetic, she thought angrily as she sniffed loudly.

'Of course you are,' he said soothingly, 'but it'll be much more comfortable if you're off that knee. Here, Jake, support her around the waist and we'll turn her over.'

Anna felt the touch of competent hands.

'After three—ready, Anna?' She nodded.

The manoeuvre was completed swiftly, and Anna was sitting on the ground able to view the world from a more conventional angle. Seeing at a glance all the faces peering at her, she wrapped her arms instinctively around herself. 'I feel like an idiot—and I'm not your patient!'

'Cheap publicity stunt!' a loud voice blustered. 'My driver was in no way responsible.'

'Get rid of the pompous idiot, Jake.' Adam flashed a fierce, irritated look over his shoulder.

'My pleasure,' the young man agreed cheerfully, getting to his feet. He gave Anna a broad smile, and with a ruthless look in his eyes reminiscent of his uncle he moved purposefully away.

'Your nephew?' Anna asked as Adam pushed aside the voluminous folds of her skirts to reveal her knee. She was impressed by the young man's confidence and his uncle's obvious trust in his ability to resolve the situation.

Adam nodded, his hands moving over her leg, his fingers delicately probing the sensitive area. 'Painful?' he asked as she flinched.

'Not too bad,' she said honestly. 'I think I might have panicked,' she admitted gruffly, straightening her bonnet.

'Understandable.' Adam raised his head from his contemplation of her leg, and for the first time since the accident she looked into his face. A wave of warm emotion swept over her. Hot-cheeked and conscious of the tightening in her chest, she stared back, feeling ludicrously self-conscious.

'I'm sorry to have been so much trouble,' she said softly. He was staring so fixedly at her face that she couldn't look away. 'And I won't sue.' The milling crowd seemed to have retreated into the distance.

Adam seemed belatedly conscious that he was staring. 'Jessica was only...'

'Looking after your interests?' she suggested.

Adam didn't disagree. 'I don't think there's any serious damage but they'll know better once you've been X-rayed. That sounds like the ambulance now.'

'I was aiming for drama, but not quite this much.'

'Your period costume didn't extend to the footwear, I see,' he said, touching the trainer-clad foot which lay in his lap.

Anna touched the ruined gown with a frown. 'I promised to bring this lot back in perfect condition,' she said ruefully. 'The amateur dramatic society's new production begins on Saturday.' She blew away a troublesome feather that had become detached from her bonnet as it tickled her nose, and gave a droll grin.

'It would be more sensible to be concerned about the state of your knee, not your outfit.'

'I am concerned.'

Adam's comprehensive scrutiny took in the white-knuckled grip she had on the folds of her skirt.

'Let me guess. Your fertile imagination is already conjuring up interesting limps and wheelchairs?' Adam noticed her shiver and placed his jacket around her shoulders. 'I don't like to outguess the tests, but I'm willing to say there's no permanent damage.'

Anna hunched her shoulders, feeling the second-hand warmth of his body through the fabric and wishing foolishly that it was direct contact that was giving her the warm glow. The man was painfully astute. Losing her mobility had always been one of her most vivid nightmares, especially as she knew how close she had come to it once.

Anna expected Adam to disappear when the ambulance men arrived, but to her surprise he announced his intention of coming with her.

'That won't be necessary,' she said stiffly. Panic rose because she did want him to come; she wanted it quite badly. Weak and helpless doesn't suit you, Anna, she told herself severely.

'No, it won't; I'll go with Anna,' Simon announced, with a belligerent expression on his normally good-natured face.

'Thank you, Simon.' She smiled her gratitude. She wasn't up to being with Adam in the close confines of the ambulance; she wasn't up to being with him anywhere!

'I have to deliver the patient to my colleague, give a medical history—'

'I'm not dumb,' Anna interrupted.

'It's a courtesy,' he said tersely. 'Perhaps your *friend*—' Anna put a restraining hand on Simon's arm as he bristled at the sneer in Adam's voice '—might be better employed telling your parents what has happened.' He tossed the car keys to Jake, who had reappeared. 'Drive back to the hotel. I'll see you there later.'

'Jessie has a meeting first thing in the morning; she won't be happy,' his nephew observed.

'She'll have to catch a train up to town,' Adam said impatiently. 'Where is she, Kate?' he asked as his niece reappeared with the twins in tow.

'The boys couldn't wait for a toilet. I'm afraid she's overcome by the social stigma of it and has sought refuge in the Range Rover.'

'It's locked,' Jake said. A faint grin touched his lips as he imagined scarlet fingernails hammering on the paintwork.

'Too late,' one of the cherubs said cheerfully. 'She won't die like Mummy, will she?' His round eyes were on Anna, now made comfortable on the stretcher.

'She won't,' Adam said calmly.

Anna could see the child accepted his word as something indisputable in his turbulent young life. She found she was deeply moved by this small display of faith, and found herself wistfully imagining how nice it would be to feel that way.

'I shall be back later,' Adam said, catching Kate wiping a tear from the corner of her eye. 'We'll drive back to Granny's in the morning. You do as Jake says.'

'Anna?' Simon hung on, determined not to be so easily dismissed.

'I'll be fine,' she said, grinning to offer proof of this claim. 'Tell Mum and Dad for me, but don't let them panic,' she pleaded as the stretcher was lifted.

'I don't need you, Adam.' Anna's voice carried

clearly on the breeze as they moved towards the ambulance.

'Temporarily, you're stuck with me,' came the intransigent reply. 'So give your mouth a rest.'

'Don't you ever listen to anyone?' she asked wrathfully. 'And if you think I'm being treated by you…'

'I've no more wish to be your doctor than you have to be my patient,' he assured her from between gritted teeth.

'I suppose you think I should be grateful.'

'I never have had much faith in miracles. That's more your field, isn't it? Shall I sprinkle you with sweet-smelling oils and pour some herbal remedy down your throat? Would that make you happy?'

'Thank God not all doctors are narrow-minded bigots,' Anna hissed as the ambulance door closed.

Kate looked at her brother, a speculative smile playing about her lips. 'Are you thinking what I'm thinking?'

'When Adam is mad he's always devastatingly polite—he's *never* rude,' Jake reflected. An expression of pure pleasure spread over his face. 'Did you hear him with her?' he said wonderingly. 'I've never seen anyone get under his skin like that before, have you?'

Kate shook her head. 'He *never* yells at Jessica. Did you see her face back there when he just snapped at her?'

'All that well-bred civility gives me a headache,' Jake confided with an expression of disgust. 'Who *is* she?' he asked curiously.

'She's definitely the toothbrush lady; I recognised her voice.' Kate gave her brother a slow smile. 'Maybe she's also the answer to our prayers.'

'Don't pin your hopes on it, sis,' Jake advised soberly. 'She looked a bit young for Adam.'

Kate gave her brother a pitying look. 'No woman will *ever* think Uncle Adam is too old. Besides, you were too busy looking down her dress to notice her face. Men are so disgusting!' She gave a haughty sniff.

Jake grinned unrepentantly. 'I think you're meant to with those dresses,' he said, obviously considering the occupation a legitimate one. 'She didn't seem like Adam's type to me, and I still think she's too young for him.'

'Too old for you,' Kate informed him maliciously. 'Uncle Adam's seriously dishy. You ought to hear some of my friends on the subject. Honestly, Jake, he needs someone with a bit of—I don't know—spirit, to make him laugh occasionally.'

'He wasn't laughing,' her brother reminded her. 'In fact when she walked in front of that car I thought he was going to murder someone—probably her.'

'You know what I mean,' Kate responded impatiently. 'He *never* laughs with Jessie and if he does she manages to remind him that such behaviour isn't in keeping with his role as a consultant surgeon. The woman's a real pain in the posterior!' she reflected grimly. 'Did you hear her going on about boarding-schools being superior? It doesn't matter for us—we're almost ready to leave home—but for the twins' sake we can't let Adam go through with it.'

On this subject both siblings found themselves in complete agreement.

Two hours later Anna sat in the foyer of Casualty, waiting for her father. Her knee was immobilised in a thick, unattractive bandage and a pair of crutches was propped up beside her wheelchair. Her outfit was attracting a good deal of attention and a few sniggers. She wished she had something to cover her exposed cleavage.

To her relief Adam's diagnosis had been confirmed. The swelling would go down fairly rapidly. Rest and painkillers were the only things she'd been prescribed.

'I thought you'd gone home.' The squirmy mess in

her stomach made her feel sick as Adam silently materialised. He belongs to someone else, she told herself firmly. Polite but distant is what I'm aiming for.

'I've got a taxi outside.'

'Simon will have got Dad to come for me.' Her confident smile faded as he replied.

'While you were being treated I rang your parents to reassure them. They agreed that as I was passing we might as well make the journey together.'

'I don't suppose it occurred to you to ask me?' she said witheringly. This was like some ghastly conspiracy. If she ran away to the Sahara she would probably bump into him!

'I knew you'd say no, just for the hell of it.'

'It could be I don't enjoy your company,' she suggested sweetly. If he knew the half of what his company did to her...!

'Suffering is good for the soul, or so I've heard. Anyway grab your crutches and we'll be off,' Adam said, dispensing with discussion and bending to sweep her up.

'What do you think you're doing?'

'I'd have thought that was self-evident.' He spoke with his arms full of her. 'Will you do something with that hat?' he added as the feather trim prickled his nose.

'Don't tempt me,' she said darkly, valiantly keeping up the pretence of hating this manhandling.

Actually it was a novel and incredible experience to feel the strength of his arms around her. She wasn't helpless and didn't need cherishing, but... He gave her a quizzical look and she cut off a tremulous sigh. She closed her eyes; she didn't want to let the fact that this was all illusion spoil the experience. He smelt quite marvellous—warm, spicy and, well, male! Give me strength not to do anything obvious like burst into flames, she prayed.

When they reached the taxi Adam gave directions to

the driver and, after sliding her into the back seat, joined her. 'There's no room for you.'

'Yes, there is, see? Legs elevated,' he said, placing her feet in his lap.

The painkillers were making her feel slightly drowsy and the motion of the car made her eyelids feel heavy. 'Your nephew, Jake, looks like you,' she said brightly. Adam looked tired, she realised with a spasm of guilt. He had enough on his plate without nursemaiding her. The fact she was enjoying it made her guilt stronger.

'You want to make small talk? Fine.' He shrugged. 'Jake looks like his father and people used to see the resemblance between us.'

'I thought he'd be younger.'

'He's almost nineteen—off to university in the autumn. He spent last year back-packing across Europe.'

'He seems very competent.' Perhaps that too was genetic.

'He's apt to take too much responsibility on his shoulders.' This observation brought a worried frown to Adam's brow.

'That's only natural, given the circumstances.'

Adam nodded. He didn't seem to be aware of the fact that his fingers were running up and down her slim, uninjured calf in slow, circular motions. Anna wished she could be equally oblivious to the casual contact which was sending darts of sensation over her tingling leg.

'He's young. I don't want him tied down with responsibility, and Kate is nearly as bad. The twins turn to her as a mother replacement.' A glance from his heavy-lidded eyes made her revise her opinion—there was nothing unconscious about the light caress of his fingers.

'No doubt Jessica will lift the load from her shoulders,' Anna observed neutrally. 'That was the plan, wasn't it?' She couldn't prevent the edge of scepticism from creeping into her tone. She couldn't put a face to the name, but the cool, perfectly modulated but strangely featureless voice had remained clearly in her mind.

'Jessica is trying very hard—and the twins can be *very* trying.'

'They're gorgeous,' she said warmly, recalling their cherubic innocence.

'They were like kids themselves starting all over again with the twins,' Adam recalled. 'Ben and Tessa.'

The bleak expression that passed over his features made Anna's tender heart tighten in her chest. 'They have you.'

Adam shot her a startled look. 'I'm hardly parent material.'

'I've already told you once, you have potential. Have you forgotten?'

'I probably haven't forgotten *anything* you've said to me.'

She reacted to this unexpected admission with a rush of words. 'No one's born a parent; it's something people learn as they go along. Mum and Dad had given up hope of ever having children when we came along and they coped with the three of us. You're bound to make mistakes. I just don't think you should be so hard on yourself,' she finished lamely.

What had he been trying to say? *Why* had he remembered everything she'd said? Could it be the impact she'd made on him wasn't as superficial as she'd imagined? Get real, Anna, she told herself brutally. The only thing he wants from you is your body! Sometimes being brutal was the only thing that stopped her making a total fool of herself.

'You're the last person in the world I'd expect such a glowing character reference from,' he said, looking at her with an odd expression.

Her eyes slid away from the intent stare. She was very conscious that she'd sounded overly fervent. She shrugged. 'Being a parent is a job for amateurs. Your problem is you're too much of a perfectionist.'

'Wouldn't *you* be daunted by the prospect?' His words brought her head up with a snap.

'It's not something I've given a lot of thought to,' she admitted.

'I don't suppose you give *anything* much thought.' The corners of his mouth turned down with disapproval. 'Take that farrago this afternoon.'

'I'll have you know a *great deal* of thought went into that farrago,' she retorted huffily. 'Organised chaos requires very careful timing, and a bit of prayer doesn't go amiss,' she added with the faintest twinkle in her eyes. 'I'm very pleased with the way things went. Except for this bit.' Her gaze shifted to her bandaged leg.

'You mean that wasn't deliberate too?' he mocked. 'Plucky crusader risking her life to rescue elderly protester from the jaws of death?' he suggested. 'That media circus must have loved it.'

'You really do think I'm a complete crackpot, don't you?' Her voice rose to an indignant pitch. 'As if I'd pull that sort of stunt! When you're fighting against the odds you have to do things that capture the imagination just to get your case heard. I wish it was easier to raise public consciousness—'

'Save the lectures.' He leant forward and placed a finger lightly against her parted lips. 'What happened to your sense of humour? I was teasing.'

Achingly conscious of the impression his finger had left against her mouth, she regarded him suspiciously. 'My sense of humour is fine, thank you. It's the fact that *you* have one that leaves me speechless.'

'Ouch!' He winced. 'I take it that that show back there was your baby?'

'A lot of people are just as committed...'

He made an impatient gesture. 'You wrote the script and directed the action?'

'What if I did?' She suspected her admission would unleash a fresh torrent of criticism.

'I've never met anyone with so much stamina—mental and physical,' he mused. His grudging admiration threw her off balance. 'You really are a sucker for a lost cause.'

'I like to win occasionally.' One day she might convince him to stand up and be counted, she thought, forgetting for the moment that she wasn't going to have anything to do with Adam Deacon ever again.

'Is that what your Simon is? He's a loser.'

'Simon is not a loser,' she contradicted him, her eyes flashing angrily at this sly dig. 'You don't know him, and he's not mine.'

'He let me come with you to the hospital, didn't he?' Adam reminded her, his expression making it clear he despised the younger man for being so easily out manoeuvred. 'I know his type,' he continued with a surprising amount of venom. 'He relies on his schoolboyish looks and charms and has cultivated the helpless look that has all your maternal instincts screaming to look after him.'

'I don't feel the least little bit maternal as far as Simon is concerned,' she informed him with a gentle, sphinx-like smile.

The heat behind his hostile glare was vaguely shocking but also satisfying. It made her feel less impotent to know she could still hold her own verbally when so much was outside her control.

'So you've dropped the ''just good friends'' story, have you?'

'I've known Simon most of my life and I value his friendship. He's kind, steady and he doesn't make snap character judgements.' To her dismay an evil voice in her head added, Boring, and she heard herself adding defensively, 'Possibly because *he's* not an arrogant pig with an over-inflated ego. He...' The rest of her statement was lost in the warmth of his mouth as he leant across and kissed her full on the lips.

'He'd never dream of doing anything so despicable,' Adam said huskily as he lifted his head a little from hers.

It occurred to him that not very long ago he could have claimed the same thing himself. Something about this woman made him override his principles, the precepts he'd conducted his life by. 'Keeping you at arm's length is getting beyond my control.' The admission was bitter.

Anna's eyelids felt heavy as she lifted them to look into his face. She could see the fine tracery of lines radiating from the corners of his eyes, appreciate the texture of his lightly tanned skin.

'No, I don't think Simon would,' she agreed, a husky catch in her voice. She caught her trembling lower lip between her teeth. 'My sister's in love with you.' I really will have to do something about this communication problem between my mouth and brain, she thought grimly.

'Which one?' He stroked the curve of her cheek with his thumb.

'Don't be smart.' She continued to fight with all her might against the hypnotic pull of his eyes. Now it was out in the open she wasn't going to let him laugh it off.

He did laugh in what she considered a heartless manner.

'It's no joke. I'm surprised you didn't interview her for the job of wife and mother; she's a much better catch than Jessica!'

'I'm flattered that you think she'd be interested, but Rosalind and I have a strictly professional relationship. She's a very single-minded lady and I'd have noticed if there was anything else on the agenda. It would have interfered with our working relationship, and I couldn't have allowed that.'

It sounded pretty ruthless to Anna but she didn't mention this fact. It was hard enough to concentrate on the main theme of their conversation without introducing any sub-plots.

'How can you be so sure?' Could she have misinterpreted her sister's distress?

'Did Lindy say she was in love with me?'

'No...but—'

'What did she say?'

'She said she missed you and she's having trouble adapting to her new boss.'

'How exactly did this translate as an avowal of love?' he asked scathingly.

When he put it like that she did see there was a possibility she'd read more into the conversation than had been there. 'She sounded so...so emotional. Lindy doesn't get emotional. Well, she does, but she hides it.'

'Unlike you,' he murmured drily. 'Listen, Lindy's great at her job. I'd have had no hesitation in giving her the registrar's vacancy that's coming up soon. It takes time to adapt to a new way of doing things, and I'm sure my successor is eager to stamp his own personality on the job. Maybe Lindy is feeling resistant. It's possible she has looked on me as a sort of role model.' He gave a self-deprecating shrug. 'I could have a word with Steven—'

Anna felt a rush of relief. 'No, don't interfere. Lindy's very independent. Do you really think that's the problem?' It had been pretty awful feeling jealous of her own sister and angry on her behalf at the same time. She was ashamed to admit that the jealous part had been the stronger of the conflicting emotions.

'I was pretty strongly influenced myself by someone in my early days. If it hadn't been for his encouragement I'd have walked away from medicine at a very early stage. Angus Montford was an inspiring teacher and a good friend.'

'Was?' she said softly. There was a sadness in Adam's

face that cut her deeply. She wanted to believe his explanation. She didn't want to think of her sister suffering as much as she was, but she didn't feel Adam could be compared to an elderly mentor.

'Angus died three years ago. Jessica is his stepdaughter,' he said stiffly.

A feeling of hopelessness washed over Anna. The stepdaughter of a man Adam considered he owed his career to. He would never leave her for the sake of a passion he regarded as nothing more than temporary insanity. She couldn't compete, but then she'd always known that so it shouldn't hurt this much.

'You've known her for a long time, then?'

'Actually I'd never met her until the funeral. She was devastated.'

'And you comforted her.' It made Anna feel sick, imagining the form that comfort had taken. 'Odd you'd never met her before if she was such a devoted daughter.'

'There's nothing odd about it,' he said tersely. His expression made her feel small and mean-minded. 'It made a difference at the time that there was someone else who had known Angus well and missed him. He was an extraordinarily perceptive man with a great mind.'

'Perhaps I did jump to conclusions. I'm sure Lindy would have more sense than to get involved with someone who's already spoken for. It's not a formula for happiness.'

'Very subtle,' he said admiringly in a tone that made her flush. 'But there's no need to be subtle at this stage in our acquaintance, Anna. There's no perhaps about it—if Lindy has lost her heart, it's not to me. A man always knows when a woman is in love with him.'

'He does...?' This was bad news, she thought, closing her eyes. Was he trying to tell her that he knew?

'I know you don't love your Simon.'

Anna gave a sigh of relief which was submerged by a flash of anger. 'You also know you don't love your Jessica!' She caught hold of his hand and removed it from the side of her face. If he could be personal so could she!

'Jessica cares enough about me to give up an offer of a job in New York, a job she's always wanted. When I needed her she was there.'

'And you're proving how grateful you are by making love to me,' she choked. She still held his hand pressed between her two smaller palms.

'Don't you think I've told myself that? For pity's sake, Anna, have you any idea what you did to me when I saw you go under that car?' He closed his eyes and shuddered as if reliving the incident. 'I know it's crazy to feel this way,' he groaned, cupping her face in his free hand.

Anna felt choked with emotion. 'I don't want the dregs, Adam.'

'You expect me to reject Jessica after all the sacrifices she's made for me and the children?'

'I expect nothing from you except to be left in peace!' she told him with quiet dignity.

Not surprisingly the rest of the journey was completed in stony silence. On their arrival at Anna's parents' home, one look at Adam's profile silenced her protest as he scooped her up into his arms and strode up the path to the farmhouse.

Her parents greeted her with so much warmth and concern, she felt her eyes weakly fill with tears.

'You wouldn't believe how many people have been ringing, asking about you. You're the local heroine,' her mother said.

'Hopefully that won't take long to wear off.'

'I'd have thought you'd have lapped up the publicity.' Adam treated her grimace with a look of disbelief.

'That's it, put her down there, son,' her father en-

couraged Adam, who laid her on the sofa. 'We've just
been watching you two on the local news. Well, Anna
mostly, although they had managed to dig out your cre-
dentials as the doctor who was fortuitously on the scene.'

'Enterprising.'

Anna could see he wasn't exactly enthusiastic about
his moment of fame. He'll probably blame me for that
too, she thought bleakly.

'You've got your moment in the sun too,' she said.
'It just so happens I wasn't seeking to thrust myself into
the limelight either, just the issue.' He couldn't be more
wrong if he imagined she relished her up-front role.

'Sit yourself down; we're very grateful to you,'
Charlie Lacey said.

'I can't stay. I've got a taxi waiting and my fiancée
has had sole charge of my niece and nephews all afternoon. Above and beyond the call of duty.'

'Have you all been staying at the Rectory?' Beth
asked, having satisfied herself that her daughter's inju-
ries really were as superficial as Adam had told them on
the phone.

'A hotel; things are a bit too primitive at the house at
the moment.' He didn't add that Jessica's praise of the
house had been strained, to put it mildly. 'The builders
are in next week, though there's not much wrong with
the place structurally. The sooner we can move in the
better. The children are staying with my mother just
now, but she's not young. It's only a temporary solution
at best.'

Beth nodded sympathetically, not pretending that the
intricacies of his personal situation were unknown to her.

'Well, thank you for putting yourself out on Anna's
account. Simon told us all about it.' She exchanged a
quick, amused look with her husband that left Anna
wondering what exactly 'all' had been. 'You've only just
missed him. We finally persuaded him to go home. I
thought it best; Anna hates being fussed. She gets

quite…ahem…astringent,' she said, ignoring her daughter's squeak of protest. 'But then perhaps you've already noticed that.'

Adam wisely didn't comment. 'Goodnight, Mrs Lacey, Mr Lacey.' His hand was heartily wrung by her father.

'Thank you, Adam, dear,' Beth said warmly. She looked pointedly at her daughter, prompting her to remember her manners.

'Thank you,' Anna managed gruffly. The 'Adam, dear' hovered in the air. She badly wanted to know how it would feel on her tongue.

To her surprise Adam bent down, his hand on the back of the sofa, to brush her forehead with his lips. 'Don't make a habit of throwing yourself under the wheels of cars, will you?' His words initiated a ripple of laughter, but Anna had seen strain, not humour in his eyes as he'd leant close.

'I don't hold out much hope,' she heard her father say as the mobile members of the small assembly moved into the hallway. 'That's always been Anna's problem—she never did think before she did anything.'

I've really surpassed myself, Anna thought dismally. I've fallen in love this time, and no amount of thinking after the fact is going to alter that!

CHAPTER SIX

AFTER two days of hobbling along on crutches Anna was almost screaming with frustration. Never blessed with patience, she liberally inflicted her ill humour on the rest of the household.

'Is it just your leg that's making you so unpleasant?' her mother asked after suffering another of her daughter's outbursts. 'Or is that just a convenient excuse?'

'What's that supposed to mean?' Anna propped her crutches against the dresser and reached up to replace a china plate. She knew she was being impossible. She felt guilty for being such a pain, but no matter how hard she tried she couldn't snap out of it.

'I mean are you really being so vile because your wings are temporarily clipped, or is there some other reason?'

Anna hooked the crutches back under her arms and swung herself across the room. 'I'm sure I'll regret asking this,' she said resignedly, 'but what other reason did you have in mind?'

'Adam Deacon?' Beth's eyes were filled with sympathy as her daughter's face went fiercely hot and then deeply pale in rapid succession.

'Adam Deacon has nothing whatever to do with me.' From her mother's expression Anna could see she might as well have denied her eyes were brown. Her mother hadn't referred back to the embarrassing incident before and Anna wished she hadn't now. Pity was the last thing she wanted!

Beth Lacey gave an unruffled smile and wiped the excess flour from her hands onto her apron. 'If you say

so, my dear. I always thought you were more of a
fighter.'

'Fighter! In case you'd forgotten, Mother, Adam is
almost a married man.' Anna's teeth clenched against
the sob of frustration in her throat.

'Almost.'

'Mother!'

'Sometimes fate has rotten timing, child.'

'Is it really that obvious?' Anna asked huskily, aban-
doning pretence.

'Not to him perhaps. Have I said something funny?'
she asked as Anna began to shake, her laughter tinged
with hysteria.

'Obvious is exactly what Adam thought me when we
first met. I haven't actually given him much reason to
revise his opinion.' Her lips twisted in an ironic smile
as she recalled their first meeting.

Nothing had gone right since she'd met Adam, Anna
reflected gloomily. First her direct approach had been
misinterpreted and she'd succeeded in alienating him.
When he had finally decided to follow his instincts she'd
discovered she wanted a lot more than a brief fling.
Great timing!

Adam obviously set a lot of store by his integrity, and
it was obvious to Anna he held her responsible for his
moral lapse. It seemed Adam Deacon didn't allow himself to become as human as everyone else. When the
sexual attraction he felt for her had dissipated he would
probably be grateful that nothing had happened. She
could only hope that she would be too.

That afternoon Simon chauffeured her to the small consulting room she leased in town. She could at least catch
up with her paperwork even if she'd been obliged to
cancel all her appointments for the week.

When she'd got what she'd come for she found him
curiously examining the small consulting room. She'd

built up a small but growing clientele, and her relationship with the local medical practice meant she was frequently sent patients they thought might benefit from treatment.

'I see you're wired for sound,' he observed, looking at the speaker system housed in niches around the walls.

'Music, soothing lighting and the correct atmosphere are important,' she explained, smiling as he took the file she was balancing.

'I might give it a try.' He flexed his shoulders.

'For you it would be on the house,' she said lightly.

This new Simon did seem to have kinks in his spine. He certainly didn't have the carefree attitude of the boy she'd once known. But then he wasn't a boy any longer, she reminded herself.

'We'd better be off.' Her casual comment had made him look at her in a way that made her feel vaguely uneasy.

God, but I'm fickle, she thought, locking the door behind her. Once upon a time I'd have given anything to have Simon look at me like that, and now... With a sigh she carefully negotiated the flight of stone steps. Simon stood at her elbow, offering advice and constantly admonishing her to take care. She didn't receive his concern with the gratitude it warranted; she just felt a sense of increasing irritation.

'Hello, there!' For a moment the green eyes made Anna's breath freeze. 'I don't know whether you remember us?'

'Yes, of course,' she said, quickly flicking a quick glance to either side. Her breathing slowed. No sign of Adam, just his charges. You're being ridiculous; it doesn't matter if he is here. Act your age, girl, she admonished herself sternly. 'This is Simon...'

Jake nodded easily in the direction of the older man but kept his attention firmly on Anna. She found she wasn't offended by the overt curiosity in his eyes. There was something very engaging about this young man.

'My name's Jake.' He extended his hand, and then laughed when he realised she didn't have a free hand. 'This is Sam and Nathan,' he said, extending the introduction to his two small charges.

Anna didn't flinch under the unblinking regard of two identical pairs of eyes. The only way to differentiate between them she could detect was a large brown stain over Nathan's white T-shirt.

'Hello, boys.'

'Uncle Adam said you wouldn't die,' the owner of the clean T-shirt commented.

'He's a doctor, he fixes people,' the other added.

'Adam's giving the local schools the once-over with Kate,' Jake explained. 'We're sort of at a loose end for an hour or so. I thought we'd explore the town, but these two need feeding and watering every twenty feet or so. Do you know anywhere that sells ice cream?' he asked appealingly.

Whilst he was more than capable of taking care of his brothers Jake knew when a little male helplessness was called for. On cue the twins started chanting, 'Ice cream,' in piercing voices.

'Tell you what,' Anna said, 'why don't I show you where the tea rooms are? They do chocolate fudge cream sundaes to die for.' The look of gratitude on Jake's face made her glad she'd made the impulsive offer. She wondered with an aching heart whether Adam had ever had such an ingenuous, open expression in his eyes.

'We don't want ice cream,' Sam said, literally digging his heels in and tearing his hand from his brother's grasp.

'I do,' his traitorous twin announced.

'She said you have to *die* for it,' came back the hissed reply.

Anna exchanged a stricken glance with their elder

brother. 'I'm sorry.' She was appalled at the result of her inadvertent comment.

'Don't worry, they're at the literal stage,' Jake replied calmly. 'Death is by way of being the taboo word just now,' he explained. 'The lady just meant the ice cream is excellent. It's quite safe; nobody is going to die. The lady will come with us,' he added to his half-convinced brothers. 'Won't you?'

It would have taken a harder heart than Anna possessed to resist the appeal. 'Simon?'

'I've got to get back, love,' he said, not looking delighted at the turn of events. In fact she discovered he looked faintly sulky. 'Tell you what, I'll pick you up in an hour.'

'You don't have to do that.' She was already chafing against her temporary loss of independence.

'It's no bother.'

Anna offered her cheek as he bent his head, and was startled when he kissed her mouth instead. She turned to find Jake watching her with an expression of disapproval that was so uncannily similar to his uncle's that she found herself blushing guiltily.

Some ten minutes later, when they were all happily installed in the tea rooms, Anna allowed herself, against her better judgement, to be talked into having a confection that required a foot-long spoon to get to the gooey bottom of the glass.

'Bit on your nose,' Jake told her with a hint of apology as she scraped the last remnants from her glass.

'Thanks.' She wiped the tip of her nose with her napkin.

'Better,' he approved as she offered her face for inspection. 'When Jessie sees this pair she'll probably faint.' He regarded his grubby brothers with a tolerant eye.

'She's here too?' Anna was unable to keep the dismay from her voice.

The young man gave no sign of noticing anything amiss in her reaction; he nodded. 'She doesn't let Adam out of her sight for long,' he said sourly, with a thin-lipped smile.

Anna didn't know how to respond safely. Nobody could accuse her of being unbiased on the subject!

'People like to be together when they're in love.' Considering how eaten up she was with jealousy, she gave herself ten out of ten for selfless generosity!

'In love!' Jake scoffed. 'Uncle Adam doesn't love her.'

'I don't think Adam would like it much if he knew you were discussing him with me,' she said uneasily. Well, she could hardly agree with him, could she?

'It's just I feel so damned responsible. If it wasn't for getting lumbered with us he wouldn't...'

The anguish in the young man's eyes brought a frown of concern to Anna's smooth brow. 'You mustn't feel like that,' she said sincerely, her heart going out to him. 'Your uncle's quite capable of making his own decisions.' Even if they are all wrong! she added silently.

'You don't know Jessica,' Jake said darkly. 'She played on his doubts about his ability to give us a decent home and came over all caring and concerned. Mum always said she was more tenacious than the rest,' he reflected bitterly.

'The thing is, Uncle Adam got his fingers pretty badly burnt when he was at medical school. I can't imagine it, but Dad said he was completely besotted with this girl...well, woman actually. He refused to believe his friends when they tried to warn him she was just playing with him.

'To cut a long story short she hurt him pretty badly. He became pretty cynical about involvement after that. I gather he's not been a monk, but all the women have been like Jessica—self-sufficient, invulnerable and most importantly shallow and superficial.'

Anna took a deep breath. 'I don't think you should be telling me any of this,' she said earnestly, laying a comforting hand over his on the table. The idea of Adam being young and vulnerable took some adjusting to. Was this the time Adam had almost given up medicine? she wondered. It seemed very likely. There had obviously been more to the incident than simple infatuation. Did he still dream of his mystery woman?

'Sorry, but sometimes it's easier to talk to a disinterested party,' he confessed with a smile.

Anna felt as if guilt was written clearly all over her face. I've been greedily digesting every snippet of information he has fed me, she thought. She was horrified at the position of confidante she found herself in.

'You're right, I've no right to unburden myself to you.'

'It's not that—' she began. Her words were cut off as the twins managed to knock their drinks over in what looked suspiciously like a rehearsed manoeuvre. They giggled as the liquid dripped noisily onto the tiled floor and soaked the white linen tablecloth. A pair of deeply polished leather shoes appeared amongst the widening pool, and Anna's eyes travelled slowly upwards.

'So here you are.' Adam's cold glance took in the general chaos and came to rest fleetingly on the innocently clasped hands on the table.

'We've been traipsing around for hours looking for you. I do think you could have shown more consideration.'

Anna managed to drag her eyes from Adam's face to see the features that matched that bland voice. A voice that managed to imply criticism without any audible alteration of the cool monotone.

The features were just right for the voice—nothing was out of place, nothing marred the enviable symmetry, but neither was there anything remarkable in the other woman's face. Beauty *could* be insipid, and here was living proof, Anna decided uncharitably as her eyes swept over the perfectly groomed slender figure. Here was someone who would never embarrass Adam with tiresome spontaneity.

'Five minutes, actually,' Kate corrected her, referring to her watch. She moved forward from behind her uncle. 'Hello,' she said to Anna. 'Is your leg better? I never did thank you for helping us out on the phone.' She didn't pause to permit a reply. 'It's a very small town and I said they'd be eating. They do—continually.' She bent down beside her younger brothers and quietly took them to task for the mess.

'It's time we were going, darling, if we're to get back to your mother's this evening.' Anna was relieved that Jessica had deflected Adam's attention from her own face. His tight, brooding regard had made her totally inarticulate.

'Sorry about the mess,' she said, quelling the faintest quiver of her lips as she looked at the twins. 'The ice cream was my treat. It's remarkable how far they can spread it,' she added with a hint of awe.

'Is Hope Lacey *really* your sister?' The incredulity was insultingly over the top. 'When Adam told me I couldn't believe it. You don't have the same affinity for the camera, do you?' She gave a tinkling laugh. 'I watched you on the news report.'

It was rude, but Anna was used to this opening comment. 'Ain't the gene pool a peculiar thing?' she said breezily. 'Mind you, I wasn't at my best that day.'

'Could you get me an autograph? Lacey is out of this world.' Jake grinned beguilingly at Anna. 'And I don't know about not being at your best—the camera got some great shots of your cleavage.'

'For *you* I'll get her to put a very personal message,' she twinkled back, grateful for this youthful defence.

'I hope you're fully recovered now, Miss Lacey.' There was a noticeable lack of warmth in Jessica's voice.

Anna tapped the bandaged leg stretched out in front of her. 'I should get rid of this next week,' she said. 'I hope the incident hasn't given you a bad opinion of our little town, Miss…?'

'Jessica. Jessica Talbot. Do call me Jessica; I've heard *so much* about you I feel I know you quite well already.'

'Jessica,' Anna said dutifully. The muscles in her cheeks were aching from maintaining the fixed smile. 'It's normally very quiet here.'

'I was very impressed, Anna, by your little operation. I'm in public relations myself.'

'The next time we need to raise public awareness I'll have to come to you for advice.'

'Do you make a habit of doing this sort of thing, then?' Jessica's laugh held a definite edge of mockery.

Was it a guilty conscience, Anna wondered, or was it not just the demonstration she was talking about? 'If I get my soapbox out Adam will shout at me.' She fluttered her eyelashes vigorously in his direction.

She was damned if she was going to let this woman intimidate her! There was a challenging expression in the depths of her wide brown eyes as she gazed at him.

'Given enough rope, you'll hang yourself one of these days, Anna.'

Sam, sensing but not understanding the criticism in his uncle's voice, climbed onto her lap. He wrapped his chubby arms around her middle. '*I* like you,' he said defiantly.

'And I like you, Sam,' she responded warmly, ruffling the curly fair hair. His twin laid his head on her lap and she smiled. 'If it hadn't been for you two I'd have had no opportunity to pig out on ice cream.'

'Isn't that amazing, Uncle Adam?' Kate said. 'Anna can tell the difference between them already. Some people never get the hang of it.' She gazed innocently at Jessica, and Anna began to feel almost sorry for the woman.

'I've been trying to instil a few basics concerning nutrition, but then a *stranger* wouldn't know that...' The comment was accompanied by a smile of understanding warmth. The embryonic sympathy died a death in Anna's heart.

'Forbidden fruits always do hold a fatal fascination for children,' Anna observed with equal sweetness.

'Some adults have the same problem.' There was nothing ambiguous about the 'hands off' message this time.

Anna's fingers curled and she realised that with her free hand she was still clutching Jake's hand. She self-consciously released it. 'How did you know I have a sweet tooth?' she asked, rallying her composure. She was consumed by deep humiliation; had the warning been as clearly audible to everyone else?

'The chocolate moustache?' Jake suggested with a grin.

Bless the boy! 'How did it go at the school?' Anna asked, trying to keep the conversation civilised. It would hardly be fair to the children if she started a slanging match.

'The local ones aren't up to much. We'll have to broaden our horizons.' Jessica spoke dismissively.

'I went to a local school,' Anna said quietly. She was seething at the overt disdain in the other woman's voice.

'And you're into some sort of alternative medicine, I believe.' Her expression made it clear this was pretty low on her scale of social evolution. The throbbing in Anna's temple grew stronger. 'I don't think—and I'm speaking for Adam here...'

'I would; he's not particularly articulate, is he?' Anna commiserated.

'*We* wouldn't want anything like that for the children,' Jessica continued. 'He was only saying the other day how absurd all this fringe stuff is, not to mention dangerous.'

'I prefer the term "complementary",' Anna said tightly. The look she sent Adam was murderous. 'I think you'll find it's not obligatory to think for yourself at the local high school, but they do encourage it,' she admitted.

Her temper had reached sizzling point and she was having great trouble keeping her tongue in check. It was as well they then decided to go or Adam might have discovered how restrained she had been up to that point.

Chubby hands clutched at her as they said their goodbyes. The twins meekly followed Adam, who, other than giving her a curt nod, hardly acknowledged her presence at all. She wasted time in the ladies' room, waiting for Simon and gathering her wits before emerging outside.

'You took your time!' Adam growled.

The wits she'd so carefully gathered went walkabout instantaneously. 'It's my time,' she snarled back. 'If I'd known you were waiting, naturally I'd have run!' she observed with acid sarcasm. 'To what do I owe the honour?'

'Don't play the innocent, Anna. What exactly are you up to?'

'Give me a few clues. I've not the faintest idea what you're talking about.'

'I'm talking about your ingratiating yourself with my nephew—my family,' he drawled, with a hateful, as-if-you-didn't-know expression. 'Trying to exclude Jessica.'

'Ingratiating!' she echoed. Anger spilled over into her sparkling eyes and stiffened her slender body. 'I was merely being friendly. There isn't some sinister hidden agenda behind *my* actions. If they don't like her it's not my fault!'

A sceptical frown hardened his features. 'I suppose you weren't holding his hand either?' he scoffed. Anna could hear the suppressed rage throbbing in his voice. 'People say he looks like me.'

'Meaning I can't have you, so I'll make do with a

younger version? You really do have an inflated opinion of your charms, Adam Deacon!' Was he real? she wondered incredulously. 'Jake appears to be a warm, sensitive boy, a fact which made more impact on me than the superficial resemblance. For your information I do not seduce young boys! It couldn't be that you're jealous, could it?' she taunted.

'Jake is a young man, not a boy. An impressionable young man' he added, pointedly ignoring her jibe and regarding her with austere disdain.

'What am I supposed to do? Cross to the other side of the street when I see him coming just to shield him from my fatal charm?' she said witheringly. 'Just because *you* made a fool of yourself at his age don't assume he's that immature...' She stopped mid-flow, a horror-struck expression spreading across her animated features.

'All you had to do was ask. There was no need to butter up Jake.'

'I wasn't buttering up Jake! I like Jake.' Her expression made it clear her approbation didn't extend as far as his uncle. 'Besides, I was only making an educated guess. A man of your age who isn't married or committed is either gay, which you're not...'

'I'm relieved to hear that,' he said drily.

'Or,' she continued, frowning at this frivolous interruption, 'he's suffered a disillusionment which has made him afraid of commitment. Either that or they're just self-centred and shallow. I'd have said you were the latter, but from your reaction it would seem you're emotionally scarred.' She made her voice throb dramatically with fake sympathy. 'Poor old Adam; he's a sensitive soul really. I take it Jessica's stepfather stopped you dropping out at the crucial moment?

'Just think, if he hadn't, it might have been you, not me, who was the weirdo! The Establishment would have lost one of its props.' God, what a bitch I sound, she silently groaned into the awful, expanding silence. She regarded him apprehensively. With anyone else she could have retracted her rash words, but not with Adam.

'I'm amazed you've survived this long without someone throttling you.' She found his anger, quiet and subdued, more disturbing somehow than any raised voice. 'Just stop making waves, Anna. Leave my family out of this.' There was angry bitterness in his warning.

'As I said, it's not my fault they don't like Jessica,' she countered stubbornly, with a provoking smile. The sooner Adam learnt she wasn't about to sit back and let him tear her moral character to shreds every time he felt like it the better!

'There is no popularity contest,' he shot back defensively. 'Children often resent discipline.'

'Not when they know the restrictions and prohibitions originate from love.' She refused to be silenced by the deep frustration she read in his eyes. Empathy with this man was a luxury she couldn't permit herself.

His perception of the situation was wrong; *surely* he could see that? Jessica felt no pleasure in the children's company.

'Why can't you admit you were wrong, Adam?' She felt deep anger that he was stubbornly going to ruin not just his own life but hers too.

Adam placed his hands deliberately around the slender column of her white throat, the touch light, barely making contact with her skin. It was enough to send a flurry of shivery, warning sensations along her nerve-endings. Her throat was clogged with thick, hot emotion. The tension building up inside her was shattering.

She could see tiny points of moisture break out across his forehead as his fingers flexed and slid down across her back, pulling her against him. Neither noticed the crutches which fell with a clatter onto the floor.

The warmth of his breath against her lips, the musky, masculine scent of him in her nostrils stripped away her

defences. The first contact was brief, a faint grazing of
the corner of her mouth, the second a brief tug at her
full lower lip. A protesting sound escaped her lips—not
protest at the caress, but at the frustrating torture of the
expectation that he was building up inside her. Adam
seemed to be suffering torment of his own. His taut body
was racked by intermittent tremors and his face was
lined with strain.

'Adam, I...'

He responded to her gasping plea with a shuddering
groan and covered her lips firmly with his. Restraint
gone, he plundered the moist, sweet recesses with a fe-
rocity that filled her with a deep, nameless delight.

It was over too soon, their moment of mindless self-
indulgence. Taking the crutches he retrieved for her, she
bent her head to avoid seeing his expression—that one
of self-disgust he always appeared to experience after
lust overcame his better judgement where she was concerned.

Kissing him in broad daylight in the middle of town
with God knows how many people watching. I must be
insane! She shuddered, appalled at her behaviour.

'Are you all right?'

Her head jerked upright. 'No, I'm not bloody all
right!' Stupid, stupid man, what a question to ask! Didn't
he know how much agony it was for her just to be in
his company?

His fingers raked through his blond hair. 'It would
make it much simpler if you lied. Just once.' His husky
voice sent a tingle right down to her pink-painted toe-
nails. Irony lifted the corners of his lips from their grim
line. She loved his mouth—she loved *him*!

'I'm a walking social liability.'

'Limping liability.' He was recovering his composure
faster than she was, and she resented it.

She nodded, wanting to weep, but stayed stubbornly
dry-eyed. 'If we're being pedantic,' she agreed, permit-

ting herself a loud sniff. 'Go away,' she pleaded wearily. 'Go chastise your fiancée, not me; she wasn't exactly polite. Or didn't you notice that?' Jessica Talbot was a first-class bitch, but it seemed Adam was blind to that fact.

'Under the circumstances she was quite restrained.'

'What circumstances?' she asked reluctantly. Something in his expression told her she wasn't going to like his explanation.

'I told her about you.'

'I gathered that, but I take it there's more?' His enigmatic expression made her want to shake the information out of him.

'I told her I'm attracted to you—strongly. I told her that the feeling's mutual.'

He sounded so matter-of-fact. She stared at him in open-mouthed disbelief.

'You discussed me—with her!' she whispered incredulously. She felt deeply humiliated at the thought.

'She asked me about you and I told her,' Adam said flatly.

'Just like that!' He made it sound so logical.

'She was very understanding,' Adam observed in a neutral tone.

'This gets more and more unbelievable,' she shouted. 'Did she give you leave to sleep with me?'

'Don't get hysterical.'

'I'll get as hysterical as I want! My manners are not nearly so *nice* as Jessica's.' What sort of woman, she wondered, took the sort of news Adam had delivered calmly, sensibly? 'You really have struck gold, haven't you, Adam?' she sneered. 'An understanding wife; what more could a man want?'

'I don't want an understanding wife!' He ground the words out from between clenched teeth. Anna had the impression from the sudden, shocked look on his face that this was probably the first moment he'd admitted that, even to himself.

Startled, she swallowed the rush of hot words that trembled on the tip of her tongue. Go on, you stupid man, she silently urged as she gazed fixedly at his face. Adam seemed to be struggling to subdue the emotion that was plain to see on his face—a mixture of frustration and anger.

'This isn't the time or place to force the issue, Anna,' he eventually said harshly.

Just as if it had nothing to do with me, she thought indignantly. Well, maybe it doesn't, she added angrily. It was all very well for him to imply by his silence that the situation was beyond his control, but she for one didn't believe any situation was beyond Adam's control. It really *was* out of her control, however!

'I see,' she said in a dangerous voice. 'You and Jessica can discuss me, but I'm not allowed to discuss her. I've heard of no-win situations, but this would be funny if it wasn't so bloody...bloody! Oh, where's Simon?' she asked, looking around hopefully. 'He should be here.' She had to get away.

'The faithful Simon.'

'And you can get that oh, so superior tone out of your voice. At least I can walk down the street with him without being mauled.'

'Perhaps you don't deliberately provoke him.'

'A little opposition might bend that stiff neck of yours,' she said unrepentantly. 'I suppose Jessica thinks everything you say is engraved in stone. I don't! Just because you're a brilliant surgeon doesn't mean you're much good at the personal stuff.'

'Is that a fact?'

'It is,' she said, refusing to be daunted by the cold hostility in his tone. 'It seems to me not enough people tell you when you're talking rubbish.'

'A situation you've decided to single-handedly rectify?'

'I certainly wouldn't go out of my way to perpetuate the god-like-doctor myth. Here's Simon...' Suddenly she was limp with relief.

With neither of them prepared to back down Anna was never entirely sure where one of their encounters was going to lead. Not that it seemed likely she had a reputation left to salvage after that clinch. If a cat had been the only witness it would still be round the village like wildfire! Suitably embellished, of course.

'Just what is going on between you two?' Adam demanded, his gold-flecked gaze flicking disapprovingly over his shoulder before returning to her face.

'Sorry I've kept you waiting, love.' Breathless, Simon reached her side. 'Deacon,' he added, with a curt nod in the direction of the older man.

'Your timing is impeccable, Simon,' she said in a tight, clipped voice. 'I was just telling the doctor to mind his own business,' she added silkily. Talk about double standards! As if Adam was in any position to quiz her about her personal life! 'It's always an education to talk to you,' she said sincerely, swinging her crutches into action.

'Hell, Anna, what have you been doing to him?' Simon asked, hurrying after her. 'I thought he was going to... I'm parked up here,' he added, placing a guiding hand on her shoulder.

'How like a man to assume it was my fault,' she snapped, shrugging off his hand.

'I didn't mean that,' Simon said hastily. 'I just mean he looked—well—homicidal.'

'If you must know he wanted to know whether I'm sleeping with you.'

'*He what?*'

'I know, ludicrous, isn't it?'

'Is it?' He paused tensely, the key in the lock.

'I think you know it is,' she said a little sadly. The
scalding anger had burnt itself out now, and she felt the
full weight of her unhappiness. 'Listen, I don't know
what happened between you and Rachel, but I can't believe you're going to give up on your marriage without
a fight. Not unless you've changed an awful lot.'

'You don't understand.' He looked frustrated as he
came around the car to help her inside.

'Isn't that the wife's prerogative?' she said drily, accepting his assistance under sufferance.

Simon gave a wry grin as he closed the door, walked
round the bonnet and climbed into the driver's seat. 'You
know Rachel works in TV?'

Anna nodded.

'She's been offered an anchor job which means moving to the other side of the country.'

'That's it?' she said. 'You haven't stopped loving her
or she you. You just don't want to move house!'

'Don't make it sound trivial,' Simon said sulkily. 'I'm
expected to follow meekly…she didn't even discuss it
with me!' he said bitterly. 'What about Emily? She
barely sees her mother as it is.'

On balance she decided not to point out that skipping
the country hadn't been the act of a concerned parent,
but more that of a thwarted child. 'You wanted her to
turn down an opportunity like that?'

'For the sake of our marriage,' he replied in an injured
tone.

'For the sake of your pride more likely,' Anna returned impatiently. 'What's wrong, Simon, will she be
earning more than you?' She knew from his expression
that she had unearthed some of the problem. Male chau-
vinism really did rear its head in the most unlikely
places. 'It's not as if you couldn't work any place.'

Simon was an independent architect who worked on
projects all over North America. 'If you really care about
your marriage it seems to me you ought to be a little

more flexible. I know it's none of my business, but, considering you're all set to use me as a little light distraction given the least encouragement, I think I'm allowed some leeway.'

'I *care* about you, Anna.' His eyes slid away from her frank gaze.

'Good friends should be careful not to hurt one another,' she said quietly.

'If it wasn't for bloody Adam Deacon!' he growled, pushing the car viciously into gear.

'Adam has nothing to do with it,' she said frigidly. Whilst she felt at liberty to curse the man she felt indignant hearing his name taken in vain by anyone else.

When she went back to work the following week, Anna was snowed under trying to work through the backlog. She worked late most nights and made double the number of house calls she usually made to clients who weren't mobile enough to come into town. On the Friday it was almost eight o'clock before she got home.

'It's for you,' Beth said, handing her daughter the telephone the instant she walked into the hallway.

'Who is it?' she mouthed, but her mother shook her head. 'Hello, this is Anna.' She leant against the wall. All she wanted right now was a hot bath, food and an early night in that order.

'Miss Lacey, I hope you'll forgive me for ringing you, but Jake has told me about you, and I'm at my wits' end.'

'I'm sorry, who…?'

'So stupid of me—I'm Sara, Jake's grandmother. I'll get straight to the point. Adam had arranged for Jake and the children to meet Jessica at their new house for the weekend. He's in Amsterdam until Tuesday. I don't know how much you know of the situation, but I'll be frank. I blame myself…'

'Take your time, Mrs Deacon,' Anna said soothingly,

hearing the anguish in the cultured voice on the other end of the line. Hurry up! What's wrong? she wanted to yell. Adam's mother on the phone to her; what on earth had happened?

The sound of several deep breaths echoed along the line before the narrative continued. 'I told Adam quite frankly that the only way Jessica was going to find out what she was letting herself in for was for him to dump them on her, preferably somewhere she couldn't escape them—hence this weekend. She was meant to meet them at the house this afternoon.

'Jake rang her just before she set off to ask her to bring some children's paracetamol because the twins have a temperature. You know what the wretched woman does? She refuses to go there. In case she catches anything, apparently,' she said, her voice laden with disgust. 'She has a meeting next week and she can't risk catching anything! Can you believe that?'

Anna could, all too easily, but she made a neutral sound in her throat. 'Jake and Kate are alone with the little ones and you need someone to help them out.'

'I feel terrible asking you.' Some of the strain had gone from the voice. 'I'd go there myself, but I can't drive these days. I'm due to have a hip replacement shortly, but until then I rely on public transport. The soonest I could be there is the morning. Jake is a sensible boy, but I could tell he was worried about the little ones. They don't have a doctor there yet, and the conditions are a little primitive, I understand. I know this is an imposition...'

'Nonsense,' Anna said warmly. 'I'll get along there and suss out the situation. I'll get back to you later and let you know what's happening.'

'Jake said you wouldn't mind. I'm so grateful...'

It took Anna fifteen minutes to reach the Rectory. She swallowed the remnants of the sandwich her mother had made her take with her, and made her way up to the house. A lot had been done since she'd last seen the place—new window frames were in evidence and the ivy had been trimmed back to manageable proportions. An unpicturesque builder's skip filled with rubble took pride of place on the driveway. She made her way to the kitchen door and, after tapping on it, stepped inside.

The big room was a shell, the only decorations bunches of electrical wires hanging here and there from the ceiling. What had Adam been thinking of, sending them here? she wondered. Just as well Jessica hadn't come; one look at this place and she'd have started having serious doubts.

'Hello!' she called, walking into the hallway where the situation was no better than in the kitchen. She walked around a pile of timber propped up against the staircase and called once more.

'We're in here.'

Anna headed in the direction of the voice. Jake had obviously chosen the least awful room. He'd lit a fire in the grate and the twins were curled up in sleeping bags on top of two camp beds. Kate was sitting cross-legged on the floor between the two, looking harassed. Her young face bore an expression of profound relief when Anna walked in.

'Thank goodness,' she breathed. 'I think they're really ill.'

One look at the sleeping, flushed faces and puffy eyes had already informed Anna this was no false alarm. 'Where's Jake?' she asked, bending down and gently examining the first twin. She pealed back the cocoon to allow some air to cool the small body.

'He's gone to get some more wood for the fire,' Kate said. 'Here he is now,' she added as her brother walked into the room, carrying a basket of logs. 'It was going to be such fun,' she said miserably, 'camping here.'

'I'm amazed your uncle suggested it,' Anna said.

'So were we,' Jake said. 'But I expect he had something in mind; Adam usually does. Is it bad?' he asked in a soft voice as she straightened up.

'I'm no expert, but I'd say they've got mumps,' she told him.

'Mumps!' he echoed with some relief in his voice. He'd obviously been mentally constructing a worse scenario. 'I thought they'd been inoculated against stuff like that.'

'They probably have, but you can still get a mild form.'

'If this is mild I'd hate to see a bad case,' he observed feelingly. 'You should have heard them before they dozed off.'

'Speaking of bad cases, have you…?'

'Had it as a babe,' he reassured her with a grin. 'You must think I'm clueless,' he said ruefully. 'At home I'd have called out the doc, but we don't know anyone here except you. Did you mind that I gave your name to Gran? She was frantic.'

'No, I don't think you're clueless, and, no, I don't mind. The only question is, do we ask the doctor to come and see them here or move them to the farm first?'

'I love dominant women,' Jake said admiringly.

'Don't be fresh,' his sister advised sternly. 'Won't your parents mind being invaded by us?' she asked.

'My mum loves a crisis,' Anna assured them both. 'Is the phone connected?'

Jake produced a mobile from his pocket and handed it to her. 'My contribution to the crisis.'

CHAPTER SEVEN

ANNA leant back on her heels to relieve the pressure on her knees. Crawling around on the floor was a tiresome business, especially when the said floor was covered in stray fragments of plaster and rubble. She rubbed her hands on the seat of her jeans and gave a sigh.

'Where can they be?' she grumbled.

'My thoughts exactly.'

Anna twisted around with a cry of shock, and succeeded in falling back onto her behind. 'Adam! Goodness, what are you doing here?' She frowned accusingly up at the tall figure in the doorway. 'You're not meant to be back yet.' She hoped the sudden acceleration in her heart rate didn't register on her face. She felt that 'besotted fool' must be emblazoned all over it!

'I know what I'm meant to be—what I don't know is why you are here and why Jessica and the children aren't.'

She flushed. He'd made her sound like an intruder, which of course from his point of view she was. He'd obviously been looking forward to seeing Jessica.

'Didn't she tell you? Your mother felt sure she would have.' Surely Jessica had let him know the weekend hadn't gone exactly to plan?

'My mother?' he repeated in a voice that showed his tolerance level, never very high, was pretty low just now.

He looked tired, she noted. His face was pale, with the faintest suggestion of a shadow across his square jawline. Outlined against the doorway he was a tall, powerful figure. The dark formal suit he wore was

119

creased and his tie was loosened. 'I think you'd better tell me what's been going on here.'

'There's no need to be alarmed.' She scrambled to her feet.

'That sounds ominous.'

'I don't know quite where to begin,' she said, brushing down her dusty jeans.

'The beginning seems like a logical place. Don't stand there gawking like an idiot, woman.'

'I'm not,' she denied indignantly, knowing she had developed an alarming tendency to stare at him.

'What, an idiot or a woman?'

'Jessica didn't come.' That wiped the smirk off his face.

A look of anger crossed his tired features. 'Why the hell does nothing go to plan?' he asked, raising his eyes heavenwards.

Anna felt a solid lump of misery lodge somewhere behind her breastbone like a lead weight. He'd obviously hurried back, expecting to find Jessica. No wonder he looked pretty gutted at finding her instead, and she looked like a wreck. He'd soon discover that even Jessica wouldn't have looked brilliant if she'd spent all night soothing the fractious twins.

'You see, when Jake told her the twins weren't well—'

'What's wrong?' he interrupted, anxiety flaring in his eyes. 'Why didn't anyone let me know?'

'It all right,' she soothed. 'They've got mumps, but they're much better today. Jake thought Jessica was letting you know and she obviously thought he was. Crossed wires.'

'You mean they're *here*, not with my mother?'

'Yes, Jake had already come down; he didn't really know what to do.'

Adam was watching her with a strange expression. A

faint, sardonic smile curved his mouth. 'But you did, I take it.'

'Your mother was very concerned and she couldn't get down here to help.' She was annoyed to hear herself anxiously trying to justify her involvement.

'Why not?'

'Really,' she said huffily. She was appalled at this lack of filial concern. 'She can hardly drive down here if she's got a bad hip, Adam. It takes hours on the train, and at least two changes. I told her not to bother.'

'I take it my *poor*, housebound parent explained her circumstances to you on the telephone?' he drawled.

'Jake gave her my number. He couldn't think of anyone else. I took them to the farm; we've plenty of room and it's hardly fit here. What were you thinking of, Adam? The plumbing doesn't work.'

'The contractors promised me faithfully it would be finished,' he said, with a bland indifference that angered her. 'I suppose there's a good reason why you're crawling around on the floor?' His critical stare took in her creased and dusty garments.

'Nathan's left his teddy somewhere and I don't want to spend another night with him crying for it. Sam has lost his shoe, but that's replaceable. I'll find them if it kills me.'

'That might be a bit excessive. *You* were up all night with them?' he said critically.

'Not *all* night,' she corrected him. 'And I'm quite capable,' she added, stung by his reaction to the news that his precious charges had been in her care. 'I know you think I'm totally feckless, but—'

'I think no such thing,' he interrupted her smoothly, and with unusual gentleness. 'You just look washed out.'

'Well, so do you,' she countered, not exactly cheered by this information. There's no justice, she thought. I look drab, and he looks as sexy as hell with the odd extra line and shadow on that gorgeous face. 'Don't stand there glowering; help me look for Alexander.'

'Who's Alexander?' he asked with an expression of bewilderment.

'Nathan's teddy.' Her expression revealed her scorn for a guardian who wasn't in possession of such an essential fact.

'Are you always so cranky when you haven't slept?'

'Depends on the reason I haven't slept,' she retorted smoothly, casting him a maliciously sweet smile.

'Do you lose any sleep over me, Anna?' The husky purr emanated from far too close to her right ear. She stayed rigidly immobile, belatedly regretting her response.

'In your dreams, Adam.' She injected as much scorn into her hoarse voice as possible. What was this? Make do with Anna because the beautiful Jessica wasn't available? He had been insultingly, deeply disappointed not to find the other woman here. Not that I've any right to be insulted, she reminded herself firmly.

'I'm not sure my dreams are an entirely safe subject for exploration,' he mused, in a husky voice full of sexy significance. 'But I'm game if you are.' His soft breath brushed the ultra-sensitive area at the nape of her neck.

'You're engaged!' she cried out. She swung around to face him, her face filled with anger. 'Or had that fact slipped your mind?' How simple it would be to be swept away by the smoky invitation in his voice. A wave of self-revulsion swept over her.

'How could it?' he returned sharply. 'When you feel impelled to remind me of the fact every few seconds.' He closed his eyes and struck the heel of his hand against his forehead. 'I need to resolve the whole thing as soon as possible. Are you sure the local doctor isn't in cahoots with Kate and Jake, not to mention my mother?'

Anna stared at him blankly, wondering whether he'd

gone totally crazy. 'Are you coming down with a touch of paranoia?' she asked. 'Why would your mother want the twins to have mumps?'

'My mother appears convinced I'm incapable of managing my own life without her sage advice. When will everyone learn I will not be dictated to?'

'I can see you're pretty put out to have your plans ruined, but there's no need to take it out on me, or the twins. They didn't do it deliberately, poor lambs,' she added, glaring at him.

'"Put out" doesn't begin to cover it,' he snapped. 'You could make this a whole lot easier if you...'

Anna shuddered involuntarily in response to the subtle slur of arousal in his voice. 'Slept with you!'

'That's not what I mean.'

'Oh!' His words cut the ground from beneath her feet.

'Don't look so piqued. It doesn't mean I don't want to—desperately—but it wouldn't alter the situation. Things are a little more complex than that.'

'I am not piqued, I'm relieved.' She was deeply distracted. The husky intonation of the word 'desperately' kept replaying over and over in her head.

'Liar.' He spoke with unassailable confidence.

'Have it your own way, Adam, you're irresistible,' she snapped sarcastically. The truth as good a defence as any to defuse this potentially dangerous situation. 'But in the meantime make yourself useful and look for the damned teddy bear!'

Rather to her surprise he complied with her demand, and eventually he discovered a shoe on a window-sill whilst she found the bear lurking beneath a pile of timber.

'We make a good team,' he observed as, with a cry of triumph, she held aloft her prize.

'I've never pictured you as a team player.' The smile faded from her lips as she fought not to respond to the

suspicious warmth of his smile. 'More your despot type.'
Adam was the original lone wolf.

'Benevolent, I hope.'

'No such animal,' she concluded in a detached voice.
'You can follow me to the farm.'

'That might be beyond my athletic ability, unless you
drive very slowly. I came by taxi from the airport.'

'Then you'd better come with me,' she conceded un-
graciously.

They made their way out to the car and set off for her
parents' house.

'Do you always drive like this?' he asked tensely, after several minutes' silence.

'I happen to be an excellent driver.' She wasn't prepared to admit that his physical presence in the car was
making her a little more reckless than normal.

'I'm in no position to contradict that at the moment.'
He closed his eyes as she negotiated another hairpin
bend.

'I might have known you're one of those macho types
who can't bear to be driven by a woman!'

'Uncle Adam!' the twins cried in unison. Two small
bodies flung themselves at him as he walked into the
room. Kate was left balancing the board game she'd
been playing with them on her knee, and Jake paused,
his fingers above the keyboard of the piano he'd been
toying with.

'Back early?' Jake said casually as he met his uncle's
eyes over the two curly heads.

'It would seem that's just as well.' Adam surveyed
the cosy domestic scene with a wry expression. 'Did you
miss me?' he asked.

His eyes touched Anna as he spoke, and his attention
only moved on when he'd acknowledged her uncom-
fortable blush with a sly smile. What sordid little game
was he playing? she wondered angrily.

'We've imposed long enough,' he added briskly as Beth Lacey entered the room, drying her hands on an apron tied around a slim middle that belied her having three grown-up daughters.

'Nonsense,' she said warmly. 'We've been glad to help and they've been a delight.' She laughed as one twin detached himself from Adam and, with a shriek of pleasure, snatched the teddy that Anna had produced from behind her back.

'I came back with more than I bargained for,' Anna said awkwardly. 'I've just thought,' she said suddenly in a horror-struck voice. 'You have had...?' Her voice trailed away as the amused glint in Adam's eyes made her flush.

'Mumps? Yes, I have, Anna,' he told her obligingly. 'I'm touched by your concern for my fertility,' he observed solemnly.

'Uncle Adam!' Kate remonstrated laughingly. 'You'll embarrass Anna.'

'A farmer's daughter has an early grounding in such matters,' Beth said. 'It'll take more than that to make her blush.' She glanced at her daughter, who had developed a sudden profound interest in the board game. Anna kept her head bent over it and gave a grunt of assent. 'Hope was on the phone whilst you were out.'

'I missed her,' Anna said regretfully. Just now she really could have done with talking to her sisters. Hope was miles away and Lindy was working ridiculous hours in a London hospital. Just lately she'd been feeling nostalgic about the old days when they were all together.

'She's got a starring role in a film,' her mother said, her eyes sparkling with excitement. 'With Sam Rourke,' she said in a tone of hushed awe.

Kate squealed and looked acutely envious. 'Isn't he a dream?'

'That's marvellous,' said Anna. She knew her sister's ambition had always lain in that direction. Hope had always had her doubts as to whether anyone would ever see beyond her physical presence. She had turned down several roles which would have exploited her reputation and given her nothing to do but look sexy. Anna was happy someone was finally taking her sister seriously.

'You must be very proud.' Adam disengaged Sam's arms from around his neck and placed him on the floor.

'I'm proud of *all* my girls,' Beth said warmly. 'Well, Adam, I hope you won't mind sharing with Jake; we've run out of rooms. Unless you'd prefer the sofa?'

Anna bit back an instinctive denial. The thought of her and Adam sharing the same roof made all her instincts scream in protest. She sighed with relief as Adam replied.

'We really have imposed long enough on your generosity,' he asserted, glancing around the comfortable sitting room, which showed very definite signs of the occupation by his brood.

'I don't think you're being very practical, my dear,' Beth observed in her kindly way. Anna bit back a giggle at hearing Adam so patronisingly addressed although he accepted it without a blink. 'The children are much better, but hardly fit to travel. They both hit some nasty temperatures in the night.' She looked to Anna for confirmation. 'If you don't mind me saying so, you don't look up to the journey yourself.'

'A hotel…' Adam began.

'Wouldn't be happy to accept infectious children. I don't want to hear any more on the subject.'

Anna grimaced; he hadn't put up the sort of fight she would have expected of him. Somehow she would just have to get through the next few hours, she decided with stoical determination.

Adam did prove immovable on one subject—he insisted he take Anna's place on the camp bed in the bedroom the twins had appropriated.

*   *   *

Tired, but unable to make her overactive brain switch from its high gear, Anna lay awake, listening to Kate's light, regular breathing on the other side of the room.

Her parents' hospitality and the informal atmosphere which naturally prevailed when two young children were present had made the rest of the day surprisingly convivial. Adam had seemed quite at home in the unpretentious surroundings. He'd been more relaxed than she'd ever seen him in the children's company. Nobody had appeared to notice anything amiss in her own behaviour.

Her straining ears picked up the sound of a child's cry. She waited for it to stop but it rang out again. What if Adam hadn't woken? Rather than lie there wondering she decided to investigate. The door to her own bedroom was slightly ajar, and she paused uncertainly outside. Another small whimper galvanised her into action.

Barefoot, she entered the room. Adam's shape was a dark, ill-defined bulk in the shadows. She avoided the low camp bed as she moved behind the screen that temporarily separated her own bed, occupied by the twins, from his. The bamboo supports of the screen swayed as she got tangled in her own robe which was still draped across one corner. She bit her lip and stifled a cry of vexation.

The twins seemed to be asleep. She touched their brows and both were cool enough. But she jumped when Sam cried out.

'They're both asleep.'

She stuffed her fingers in her mouth to stifle the scream.

'I'm not, though.'

She stepped round to the other side of the screen. 'I didn't mean to disturb you,' she whispered back nervously.

'Good intentions count for nothing,' he said huskily. The sound of his voice made her heart race in panic, but it was the sharp, illicit thrill of excitement that made her turn to run. 'Don't go.'

'You should get some sleep,' she said sternly to the dark figure which rose up into a sitting position.

'My back's killing me on this thing.'

'I told you it was too small for you.'

'Don't sound so sanctimonious.'

'Keep your voice down; you'll wake them. Believe me, you *don't* want to do that.'

'Poor Anna, you must be tired. Did I say thank you?'

'You save your good manners for my parents,' she responded, moving closer as Nathan twitched restlessly in his sleep so that she didn't need to raise her voice.

'They're nice to me. Why aren't you nice to me, Anna?'

She snorted with disgust. 'Go to sleep, Adam.' A hand that accurately curled around her ankle stopped her flight. 'Let go, you idiot!' she whispered fiercely.

'Or what? You'll scream?' he suggested, his voice filled with a smug satisfaction that made her teeth grind. 'My back is murder. Why don't you come and take pity on me? In a purely professional capacity, of course.'

'I thought you didn't believe in alternative treatments,' she said hoarsely. The idea of laying her fingers against his skin was making her go hot all over. Her heart was pounding like a wild thing in her chest as she tried to sound prosaic.

'Think of this as an ideal opportunity to convert me.'

'I'm not that desperate for custom.'

'But I'm that desperate for sleep.'

The sheer weariness in his voice broke through the fatal chink in her armour. 'Then sleep on the sofa; I'll listen out for the boys,' she offered.

'I already feel guilty enough; I've deprived you of one night's sleep.'

A tiny sound bubbled free from her throat. *One night!*

If only he knew. 'It's not *my* fault you can't sleep,' she whispered back.

'I wouldn't sound so confident about that if I were you.' The raw edge in his voice made butterflies squirm in her belly. 'I've got to get this lot back to Hampshire tomorrow, and no doubt the twins will be travel-sick, as is their habit. Then come Monday I have to be back here to begin a theatre list as long as your arm.'

His thumb rubbed along her fine shin bone. 'On second thoughts it's probably longer than your arm, you being such a tiny thing. If you don't care about me, think about those poor, unsuspecting patients and the scalpel in my shaking hand.'

'For goodness' sake,' she said in exasperated defeat. 'I can't promise miracles.' She knelt down and reached tentatively out in the dark. Her cool fingers made contact with his skin and she jerked back as if stung. 'I can't see a thing,' she hissed, licking her dry lips and trying to compose her turbulent mind.

'Does that matter?' She heard the canvas bed move as he shifted his weight. 'I'm at your mercy.'

His words brought some very unprofessional images to her mind. Images of herself astride his powerful body... She shook her head to shake off the powerful illusions. She was glad of the cloak of darkness to hide her blushes.

'My hands are a little cold,' she said levelly, taking a deep breath and placing her splayed fingers on his back, correctly finding the base of his spine. He inhaled deeply but didn't reply as slowly she slid her thumbs up either side of his spinal column. Her outstretched fingers moved over the muscled ridges of his back, sliding firmly over his warm, satiny skin.

'You *are* tense,' she murmured, repeating the slow motion again. 'Is that all right?' she asked. Her body arched over his, intent on locating and releasing all the points of pressure beneath her fingertips.

A guttural sound of contentment was the only response she heard. Growing more confident with each passing moment, she continued to work on his back. The tactile sensations made her feel a little drunk and she rapidly lost track of time. He had a fine, strong back, straight, with no excess flesh to conceal the fine muscles from her probing fingers.

It was only when the physical exertion of the task began to make itself evident in her own burning muscles that she stopped. Adam's breathing was low and regular; any base motives he might have had had been overwhelmed by genuine exhaustion. The glow of warm tenderness that engulfed Anna took her by surprise and tears pricked the back of her eyelids. She closed her eyes and wearily began to get to her feet. She inadvertently brushed against his thigh and bit her lip, standing stockstill for a moment.

'You've got cold feet.' The sleepy accusation made her jump just as she thought she was safe.

'Go to sleep,' she said in a flat tone meant not to intrude into his semi-conscious state.

'Come and warm your feet.'

'Don't be stupid, Adam.' A hint of panic crept into her voice as she recognised the attractions of his invitation. She was particularly susceptible with the scent of his skin still in her nostrils and her hands still feeling his warmth. It would be easy to forget common sense in the cocoon of darkness. *'Go to sleep.'*

'Not until you warm your feet.' He was still sleepy, but she could hear a hint of awareness creeping into the stubborn tone.

'You'll wake the boys.'

'Then don't be stupid. Come and warm your feet.'

Alarmed by the rising volume of his voice, she made a split-second decision and slipped quickly under the light cover. She was only humouring a lunatic, she told herself soothingly. All sorts of warning lights flashed in her brain but she ignored them. She laid her icy feet against his bare calves and curled her body against his back. There wasn't much room to do anything else. She would stay there until he slipped back to sleep and then go back to her own bed.

Adam gave a grunt of contentment. 'That's better,' he breathed, his voice thick with satisfaction.

Anna stifled a shriek as the metal legs of the bed groaned under their joint weight, and her arm instinctively went around his middle. Her forearm was immediately wrapped firmly in a strong grip.

'Good girl,' came the approving comment.

He was asleep; she was reasonably sure of this fact. Lying very still, she waited for his grip to relax, as it was bound to, she told herself. She tried very hard not to think about where she was and what she could feel, but it was *very* difficult.

Adam was sleeping in boxer shorts that left very little to her riotous imagination. The firm, muscular globes of his buttocks were pressed against her legs. If she looped her left leg over his thighs she might stop herself slithering off the narrow bed. This was a risky strategy, but once she thought of it she found she couldn't get the idea out of her head. It had nothing at all to do with the fact that she wondered what the feel of hair-roughened flank would be like against her softer flesh—certainly not.

When she finally did it it felt sensational!

'Are you thinking of taking advantage of me while I'm unconscious?'

'Adam! You're asleep,' she accused, trying to remove her leg. He hooked his arm under her knee, effectively anchoring her against him.

'I'm tired, not dead!'

'I was falling,' she babbled. 'This bed's not built for two people.' She caught her breath sharply. 'What are you doing?' she squeaked. His fingers were moving upwards along the inner curve of her imprisoned thigh. She gave a faint moan as they moved beneath the hitched-up hem of her nightdress. 'I'll scream if you don't stop doing that,' she threatened weakly.

Her head twisted as his fingers sent shivery, electrically charged quivers down to her toes. She was panting, and her head sank against his neck.

'This is silly.' Her lips brushed against the side of his neck as she forced the words out. She ought to lift her head but all the energy had been sapped from her limbs. A sweet, aching desperation suffused her.

'Silly! This is sensational.' The smooth sound of his breathing had become as irregular and as laboured as her own shallow gasps.

'All that hard work I put in on your back will be ruined; you're getting all stiff and tense again.' She hoped this stern practicality would defuse this potentially disastrous situation.

The vibrations from the low, wicked chuckle that rumbled in his chest travelled up her fingertips. Her fingers flexed and pressed deeper into the dusting of fine hair that was sprinkled over his chest.

'I could show you…' His voice trailed off suggestively.

'I just bet you could,' she responded tartly. It wouldn't do at all if he guessed how her pulse had quickened. 'Don't you dare move, Adam Deacon!' she gasped as she felt his body shift. 'If you turn over…'

'If I turn over, what?' he persisted huskily.

'Didn't you know children always wake up at the wrong moment?' If she was honest that was the only thing that was preventing her from weakly succumbing to this forbidden craving. Her empty protestations weren't going to penetrate the sizzling passion that crackled in his deep voice; the truth just might. The privacy afforded by the screen was fragile, a fact she couldn't let him forget.

'Have you any idea what this is doing to me?' he groaned, after a short silence. He exhaled deliberately through his mouth, the series of short, hard gasps obviously part of the enormous effort he was making to gain control.

'I'll go,' she said swiftly. However superficial his feelings for her were there was no doubting they were powerful. She ought to be able to dismiss this as a demeaning game he was playing, but she couldn't. The constant battle with her own feelings left her far too malleable.

'You expect me to stay still for that?' he asked in a low, impassioned voice that was loud enough only for her ears. 'I want to turn around and feel your lovely slim legs wrapped around me. Your breasts are wasted pressed against my back—I want to feel them in my hands, taste them. I want to taste every inch of your lovely, lithe body. I want to hear you beg me to touch you. I want to feel you hot and silky as I enter you,' he growled softly.

'I've been imagining doing all those things since the first time you laughed at me and I've embroidered a good deal of detail into the blueprint by now,' he warned her. 'Don't try to sneak away now or I'll find somewhere to be alone with you.'

She believed him, though she doubted there was even an empty cupboard in the house tonight. One half of her wanted to beg him to do all the things his greedy, erotic voice had spoken of. Love was proving far stronger than her instinct to survive with her pride intact. Each syllable had echoed in her head, stretching the conflict within her to breaking point.

'Adam!' she breathed shakily. She wanted to add, Please, please love me! Instead she said in a small voice, 'I'll stay.'

'What an anticlimax.'

He had that much right, she thought dolefully. 'I thought you wanted me to stay.'

'I wanted you, full stop. Now don't squirm or our deal's null and void.' He grunted as she withdrew her leg and gave a regretful sigh. 'That might be for the best.'

'Why do you want me to stay?'

'I want to see what you look like in the morning.'

'I look like hell,' she warned him, rather angry he could be flippant when she felt so wretched.

Anna didn't expect to sleep, but exhaustion proved stronger than her expectations. Squashed into the niche left by Adam's body, she slept deeply.

Hearing was the first sense to return, a rustling and gentle giggling. Anna snuggled deeper under the covers and closed her eyes tight against the light that penetrated the delicate skin of her closed eyelids.

'Why is Anna in your bed, Uncle Adam?' The shrill childish voice shattered her tenuous grasp on slumber.

I couldn't have! she exclaimed silently. The prickle against her cheek was fine hair that covered a definitely masculine chest. I did—I fell asleep! Horror-filled, her eyes shot open.

'Good morning,' Adam said, his green eyes all innocence as she stared at him in a hunted fashion. She closed her eyes, wishing fervently that she could suddenly become invisible.

Other details, the sort you couldn't really ignore, became distressingly apparent to her. Like the fact she was lying half on top of him, one thigh draped over his legs again, one arm hooked around his neck, her breasts crushed against his torso, her head wedged under his chin. The fact she was only covered by a thin layer of cotton and he by even less made it quite clear he was not unaffected by the intimate contact.

'She's awake, she's awake!' two voices chirruped. 'Can we get in too?'

Anna groaned, and with a convulsive movement

rolled off him onto the floor, taking the covers with her. 'How could you?' she breathed, glaring at him wrathfully. She realised belatedly that pulling all the covers off him had been less than a good idea. He had the best body she had ever seen, or at least the only one that could make her stare like a child in a sweet shop. It could make Greek gods weep with envy!

'How could I not?' he responded, catching the sheet she flung at him with a grin. 'Kids, bathroom,' he said to the boys, who were standing on top of her bed watching the proceedings from their grandstand position. He just inclined his head to the doorway when they showed a marked inclination to linger, and the call of nature was more urgent than their curiosity. 'Admit it, Anna, you'd have been insulted if I'd been immune.'

'You're nothing but a lecherous…!' she began in an agitated voice. The rich, warm burr in his voice and the gleam in his eyes made her seriously frightened.

'I'm a man who woke up with his arms full of beautiful, soft, warm, sensuous female. Incidentally you look pretty passable in the morning. What do you expect me to do?'

'*Any* female would have done, then?' she interjected, her pride stung. Stupid, stupid, Anna, she told herself, biting her lip but finding the words impossible to retract.

'Fishing?' he suggested, sitting upright with a fluid movement that made the muscles in her stomach clench. God, but she loved to watch him…touch him too, a small, honest voice added.

'If you need to be reassured that I find you attractive we've got a bad communication problem here. I thought I'd been pretty forthright on that subject last night.'

'I'm hardly flattered that you took advantage of the situation.'

'On the contrary, I behaved with extremely painful decorum.' His eyes half closed as they slid over her slender figure, a half-rueful smile playing on his lips. 'Emphasis on the painful! I enjoyed waking up to find you plastered over me, and I did peek.' A devilish light shone in his eyes as she gave a disgusted groan. 'I'm only a weak man. I wasn't in any fit state to do anything about the situation last night.'

'That's not the way I remember it,' she said drily. 'Either way you seem to have recovered this morning.'

'You noticed that?'

'Hardly at all,' she responded dampeningly. He seemed to be entirely too smug about this situation for her liking. She cursed the flush that mounted her cheeks as a slow, intimate smile curved his lips.

'I can hardly let that slur on my manhood go unchallenged, sweetheart.'

'Adam!' she warned.

'Come and warm your…feet, darling,' he suggested. He was teasing her now and she knew it, but even so the tiny hiccups of excitement kept fluttering through her bloodstream, making her head feel light and giddy.

'This isn't funny,' she hissed. 'The twins saw us; what will they think?'

'The twins aren't out of that blissful and all too short age of innocence yet.'

'Don't sound so superior,' she snapped, placing her hands on her hips and loosing her grip on the swaddled blankets. 'The twins are likely to share that information with other people who will be less generous with their interpretation of events.'

'Does this mean your parents are likely to ask me to make an honest woman of you?' he enquired with interest.

'Be serious, Adam,' she retorted. 'If only I hadn't fallen asleep,' she wailed suddenly, sitting down crosslegged and pulling the blanket over her shoulders. 'This is so…so humiliating.'

'I think you're creating a tragedy out of a triviality,' he said, unmoved by her dejected figure. 'It's not as if we did anything—unless you took advantage of me after all?'

'Don't be ridiculous!' She shot him a murderous look.

'I thought I was the one without the sense of humour? Aren't you overreacting just a tad?'

If it had been anyone else but him she would have enjoyed the absurdity of the situation, but with Adam...

'Why did you get into bed with me anyway?'

'You asked me to,' she reminded him bitterly.

He struck his forehead with his hand. 'You mean that's all it takes?' he said in a thunderstruck voice. 'When I think of all the time I've wasted over the years—all the romantic dinners and flowers.'

'Shut up! I haven't received any romantic dinners or flowers.'

'Does that mean...?'

She would feel a lot safer if she could extinguish that gleam in his eyes. 'I got into bed with you because you were about to wake the twins, and I felt sorry for you. You were very tired,' she finished weakly.

'Oh, that makes it *much* clearer; I was a charity case.'

'You won't find the whole thing so funny if Jessica finds out about it.'

A speculative gleam entered his eyes and he rolled with sinuous grace back down onto the canvas bed. 'Do you think that's likely?' He placed his hands under his head and stared reflectively at the ceiling.

He didn't sound the least little bit bothered. In fact he sounded as if he relished the prospect! The inconsistencies of this man's behaviour were baffling.

'What is it with you two? Is your sex life together so boring that you need extra conquests?'

'Are you planning to be my conquest?' His attention switched back to her.

With a smile of sweet malice she placed her foot on the end of the camp bed. She deliberately placed her full weight on the fragile structure. The action had the desired effect of sending him slithering onto the floor in an inelegant heap. Silence would be the most dignified form of exit, she decided, making it to the door before he had an opportunity to retaliate.

CHAPTER EIGHT

SIMON arrived whilst everyone was sitting around the big farmhouse table eating breakfast. He looked taken aback to see the guests.

'Sorry to interrupt, but I need to talk to Anna.' Simon sounded like a man in the grip of strong emotions.

'Sit down and have some food,' her father suggested. 'She's hardly eaten anything yet,' he observed critically.

Anna had been hoping her lack of appetite would go unnoticed. She was sure the twins were going to innocently introduce what could be a very embarrassing subject at any moment, and her nerves were stretched taut. Kate had already looked at her very curiously when she'd returned to the bedroom earlier and she didn't want to fuel the speculation she'd seen in that young woman's eyes.

'Actually it's quite urgent, and I'd like to see Anna *alone*.'

'I've finished,' Anna said quickly. The faces around the table responded to this unusually forceful outburst with varying degrees of surprise and interest. 'Let's take a walk around the garden,' she suggested, pushing her chair away.

'Great!' Simon shot her a grateful look.

'Excuse me, everyone.' She couldn't stop her eyes from travelling towards Adam.

He sat between the twins, who each sat on top of cushions to boost them up to table level. He had lost his tailored, professional look today and was wearing a black T-shirt and jeans. The black was made for his blond hair and tanned skin, and the denim hugged his

139

lean hips and muscular thighs in a manner that made her throat grow dry and her cheeks grow pink.

He wasn't looking at her, but as if sensing the eyes on him he raised his head slightly and stared directly into her face. The look was so cold and hostile that Anna flinched from the austere regard before turning to leave. How dared he condemn her? she thought furiously. For it had been condemnation she'd read in his eyes and the faint sneer of his lips.

She tried to dismiss Adam from her thoughts as she led Simon to the walled herb garden that was her mother's pride and joy. He was emanating enough tension to make it quite obvious he was a friend in need and he deserved her full attention.

'Well?' she said, finally breaking the silence.

'I've been thinking about what you said—about my marriage. You were right,' he said in a rush.

'If only everybody had your perception,' she teased lightly, but it was easy to see Simon was not in the mood to appreciate humour, dry or otherwise. 'Can I help?' She ignored the voice that told her not to get involved.

'I was hoping you'd say that.' Simon caught her hands in his own.

'That sounds ominous,' she murmured. The distant sound of the twins' laughter was suddenly cut off and when she glanced in the direction of the sound there was nothing to be seen.

'The thing is, Anna, it's little Emily's birthday at the end of the week and I thought I'd surprise her—them both.'

'Sounds like a good start,' she said, not quite seeing how her co-operation was necessary for this scheme.

'Mum's gone to Scotland to stay with Aunt May; it's her annual holiday. She's brought in someone to look after the shop and post office. I'm the live-in tenant for the duration, for security purposes—the insurance insists.'

'You want me to house-sit?' she said with some relief. 'Is that all?'

'Then you'll do it?' A grin broke out over his face and he lifted her up in a bear hug. 'You're an angel!'

'Simon,' she squeaked with amusement. 'I've been accident-prone enough lately without adding broken ribs to the list.'

'Sorry. You do think I'm doing the right thing?' Doubt crept into his voice as he placed her back on her feet.

'I'm positive,' she responded dutifully. She was rewarded with a grin that reminded her of the boy she'd once known.

'About the other thing,' he began awkwardly. 'I'd hate you to think I'd been using you...I've always found you very attractive...'

'Forget it,' she said firmly. 'I have.'

She watched him leave a little while later and wished her own problems had such a simple solution.

'Isn't Simon coming in?' Beth asked when she went back into the house.

'Not today; he's got a lot to do,' she said, automatically taking the clean plate her mother passed her. Instead of putting it away she stared at it fixedly, her thoughts elsewhere.

'Jake's popped into the village for the Sunday papers. Lovely boy,' she added, her eyes on her daughter's face.

'What...? Mmm,' Anna agreed vaguely.

'So like his uncle.'

Anna's attention sharpened at her mother's too innocent face. 'Only in the looks department,' she responded. 'As you said—*Jake* is lovely.'

'I hope you won't send his hormones haywire by telling him that,' the voice behind her commented drily.

'Listen who's talking!' she snarled belligerently, turning around to face her tormentor. 'You're hardly the epitome of control, are you?'

'I think I'll go and help Kate and the boys pack,' Beth said, as if the antagonism that had sprung to life in the room weren't there. 'Excuse me, Adam, dear,' she murmured as she elbowed her way past his brooding figure.

'Has lover boy gone?'

'If you're referring to Simon then yes, he has.' She stared with unwilling fascination at a pulse that jumped erratically beside his mouth. For some inexplicable reason Adam was in a furious temper.

'He's not right for you.'

'Whatever makes you think I'd take your judgement as law?' Her large eyes sizzled with anger. 'Always supposing it was any of your business to begin with.'

'I'm making it my business.'

Anna was angry and confused, but even so she could recognise jealousy when she saw it. The sheer hypocrisy of it took her breath away, but not her voice.

'What is this, Adam? You don't want me, but you don't want anyone else to have me either?'

'I *do* want you.' All his anger and frustration were channelled into the stark words.

'As a bit of light relief,' she accused bitterly, 'before you get on to the serious stuff, like marrying Jessica!'

'Jessica isn't relevant in this conversation.'

'I wouldn't lay odds on that.'

He reached out and placed his hands on her shoulders. They felt as heavy and oppressive as the love she was carrying around in her aching heart. 'What exactly is Simon offering you? He is a married man.'

'At the moment,' she taunted, lifting her head and smiling with deliberate provocation into his savage face.

'And what would he say if he knew you woke up in my bed, my arms?' he asked. His hands slipped up to cup her face.

'I expect he'd laugh about it.' Her own laugh tinkled out, brittle and strained. 'After all, it was a bit of a joke, wasn't it?'

Hard-faced and remote, the colour bleached beneath his tan, Anna barely recognised Adam. All his emotion seemed concentrated in his eyes, and she flinched from the expression there. Maybe she'd gone a bit far in her efforts to repay some of the misery he was inflicting on her. Not that she could ever hurt him in the same way— you had to love someone to be that vulnerable. She'd just targeted his pride and frustrated lust.

'Is this a joke?'

Way too far, she thought dizzily as he lifted his mouth from her bruised lips a few moments later.

'And this?' he persisted thickly. His mouth unmercifully teased her lips into submission. With fatal subtlety he wrung a passionate response from her. As his head lifted she stood stock-still, mesmerised by the expression of fierce triumph in his hooded eyes. 'You're not laughing,' he observed throatily.

She angrily blinked back the sudden sting of hot tears. He could be so cruel! She moved her fingers, which had somehow become interlaced behind his back, and let her arms fall to her sides.

'I don't think I was meant to.' She lifted her reproachful eyes to his face. 'You didn't illustrate anything either of us didn't already know. All you've done is prove what I already knew deep down: you don't give a damn about me. You wanted to hurt me! You have—satisfied?' She glimpsed a startled expression on his face before she swept out of the room.

Anna threw the letter in the bin when she'd read it— Adam formally inviting her and her parents to dinner to thank them for their kindness during the twins' illness. She looked at the two childish drawings she'd preserved from the envelope and angrily wiped the tears from her eyes.

At least with her parents away she didn't have to dream up an excuse. She pulled the letter out of the

waste-paper basket just to copy down the telephone
number printed on the embossed paper. She would ring
and leave a message when she was reasonably certain
that he wouldn't be there.

Dinner with Adam! He must have known she would
refuse. She pulled on her jacket and hurried out to her
car to drive to work. She absent-mindedly waved to the
farmhand who was keeping an eye on things while her
parents enjoyed their West End show and shopping ex-
pedition.

'I'll see to the evening milking, Joe,' she called, roll-
ing down her window.

'Right you are, Anna.'

That evening she'd finished the milking and was just
about to have a nice, long, luxurious bath when the
front-doorbell rang. Who could that be? she wondered,
thinking longingly of scented water.

'Good evening.'

Anna stared. Jessica was the very last person she had
expected to see on her doorstep.

'Can I come in?'

Anna recollected her manners. 'Of course, please do,'
she said in a flustered manner that was in stark contrast
to the other girl's cool style. 'Come through to the sitting
room.' The tall young woman followed her into the cosy,
chintzy room. She looked around with a faintly patronising smile. Anna pushed a pile of magazines off an
armchair and motioned her to sit down. Her mind was
in a turmoil. What was the woman doing here?

'Are your parents home?'

'No, they won't be back until Sunday night. They've
gone up to London for a break. They still try and keep
the romance alive,' she reflected a touch wistfully.

'I'm glad to find you alone. May I be frank?'

'Have you noticed how people always say that when
they're going to say something you won't like?' Anna

murmured, perching herself on the arm of the sofa. She saw the other girl examining her overalls with an expression approaching horror. 'I've been milking,' she said. 'Cows,' she added helpfully as she received a blank look of incomprehension in return.

'I wondered what the smell was. Shall I get straight to the point?'

'I wish you would,' Anna said. The sooner you've said your piece, the sooner I can see the back of you, she thought. It wasn't just jealousy that made her dislike this woman.

'About this dinner invitation.'

'I have so many.'

The crimson-outlined lips pursed. 'The one from Adam,' she said almost reluctantly.

Had he sent her to personally get her reply? 'Ah, that one. Actually, I—'

'You'll refuse, of course.'

Anna, who'd been about to do just that, mentally back-pedalled. Am I missing something here? she wondered. 'I will?' she said equably enough.

'I think it would be the best thing all round if you did.'

'Best for whom?' Anna enquired, her heels firmly digging into the ground. Who exactly did the Queen of Sheba here think she was?

'For everyone concerned. I know Adam is grateful to your parents for stepping into the breach. He couldn't really leave you out of the invitation, but, quite frankly, from what he tells me it would be rather embarrassing for him if you came.'

'And what exactly did Adam tell you?' Anna asked with dangerous calm.

'Well, to be quite frank...'

'I think you've already warned me about that bit,' Anna responded. 'Spit it out,' she advised inelegantly.

'Adam finds the fact you're throwing yourself at him rather distasteful.'

'He said this?' Anna said faintly.

'He certainly implied it,' Jessica confirmed with a pitying smile. 'Adam's a very attractive man; a lot of women are attracted to him. You shouldn't feel too badly about it. I know he might have found you a—novelty, to begin with. We did discuss it. I just thought a word of caution might save you a lot of hurt in the long run.'

'I'm touched by your concern.' Anna intended to immediately shoot down any ideas of herself being a pathetic, love-sick fool. 'Of course self-interest doesn't arise—I mean Adam's made it quite clear that he doesn't find me attractive any more?'

The slight self-deprecating laugh grated on Anna's nerves. 'I flatter myself I know Adam well enough...'

'You certainly *do* flatter yourself,' Anna snapped, getting up from her seat. She stood there, hands on her hips, eyes blazing with temper. 'Did Adam ask you to come here? Or was this your idea? Are you sure you're not the tiniest bit threatened by me?' she challenged. If Adam had sent her she would kill him, she decided wrathfully.

'If you'd been your sister Hope I might have had a qualm,' Jessica observed, her eyes running over Anna's slight frame disparagingly. 'But you're not the sort of woman men take seriously.'

'If I'd been my sister Hope you'd have been stretched out on that rug. She's got one hell of a temper,' Anna reflected grimly. This was one occasion when she could readily appreciate that Hope's way of dealing with problems had its merits. She would love to wipe the smirk off this woman's painted face. 'Let me tell you something, Miss Talbot, *nobody* tells me what to do. Least of all you! Anyone would think you're scared of the competition.'

Two spots of hot colour spoiled the smooth matt finish

of Jessica's make-up. 'I just wanted to stop you making a fool of yourself. Adam would never take anyone like you *seriously*,' she sneered. 'He's far too aware of his position and his responsibilities.'

What an unbelievable snob this woman was, Anna thought incredulously. If she had her way she would stifle every decent human impulse Adam ever had and ruin his relationship with the children. She would re-inforce his tendency to take himself and life far too se-riously. Can I let this happen without a fight? she thought despairingly.

'If you really think that, why are you here?'

'Adam is too much of a gentleman to tell you to back off. Daddy always said he was one of life's natural gentlemen,' she reflected with a faint sneer.

'He may be the gentleman with you, Jessica, but he's a *man* with me.' Anna hammed the line for all it was worth. What am I doing, she wondered, fighting for him like some alley cat? 'What do you want to marry him for anyway? You obviously can't bear the children.'

'Children are fine when they're with a nanny or away at school. Adam will soon get bored with them around and realise that that is the best solution all round. He and I make the ideal couple. Daddy always wanted us to get together.'

'Adam will realise this with a little help from you, no doubt,' Anna commented with disgust. 'If Daddy always wanted you to get together why didn't he introduce you before he died? If your stepfather cared at all for Adam he'd have wanted to protect him from you!' Anna could easily imagine how this poisonous woman had played on Adam's sense of responsibility.

'My stepfather was a fool, but we'll keep that between you and me. I do have some influence with Adam,' she continued modestly, with a spitefully triumphant smile. 'As his wife I'll have even more. Adam likes things to run smoothly; we have a lifestyle which suits us both very well. I'm going to devote myself to him.'

'I don't think Adam, for all his faults, deserves that,' Anna reflected slowly, her glance scornfully raking the composed woman before her.

'For goodness' sake, don't make yourself any more pathetic than you already have,' Jessica drawled, an expression of distaste contorting her smooth features. 'This wholesome act with the children is nauseating and it doesn't fool anyone. I watched that video—I didn't find that too wholesome.'

'What video?' Anna asked, bewildered by this turn in the conversation.

'Play the innocent if you like,' Jessica said in an unpleasant voice. 'I don't know what you imagined to achieve by giving him that. It's not as if you can dance any more, is it?' she purred.

'Adam has a video of me dancing?' Anna said in a shaken voice.

'If you can call it that,' Jessica said with a shudder of distaste. 'It left little to the imagination.'

Anna's mind was whirling. All Jessica's allusions led her to believe Adam had a copy of her dancing the lead in a modern ballet. Jason Delaney, a new and exciting young choreographer, had created it especially for her. She'd only danced it once before her accident, and that had been at a private showing for the company. Jason had taped it himself and given her parents the video after the accident. How had Adam got it? Why did he have it?

'It was a love story,' she said faintly. *Swan Lake* it was not, but it was hardly pornography. It was a simple, sensitive story with a haunting score that had stretched her emotionally and physically as a dancer. She would always regret that she'd never been able to dance at its debut. 'I think you'd better leave now,' she said quietly, squaring her shoulders and facing her antagonist.

'I take it you are accepting his invitation?'

'With bells on,' Anna agreed steadily. This encounter had shaken her from the despairing lethargy she'd allowed herself to succumb to. 'I wasn't going to, but you've put quite a different aspect on the situation. I was going to sit back and act like the typical love-lorn heroine waiting for the hero to come to his senses and sweep her off her feet. You've reminded me that I never did fit into the classical romantic roles; my technique was never pure enough. Passionate interpretation was always my strong point.'

She laughed at the bewildered confusion on the other woman's face. 'What I'm trying to tell you, Jessica, is that you have a fight on your hands. I love Adam and you don't. Whilst he may not feel the same way about me he sure as hell doesn't need the likes of *you* in his life,' she finished, her face lit with breathless exhilaration.

'You'll regret this,' Jessica said, clearly unnerved by this outspoken declaration of war. 'Have you no pride?' she said as Anna escorted her to the door.

'You came here hoping to prey on my doubts and lack of self-esteem—but, you see, I'm *not* plagued by self-doubt and I *don't* feel inferior to you. I love Adam and you don't—you love the lifestyle and social position he can give you.'

'You know about his family, then?' Jessica asked with a bitter smile. 'I should have known. Don't think I'll give up without a fight,' she promised.

Anna closed the door on the sound of her heels echoing on the courtyard and leant heavily against the comforting solidity of the oak. She slid slowly down until she sat on the floor, her chin supported by her knees.

Well, for better or worse, she'd made her intentions clear. Jessica wasn't sure how much of what she'd said was bluff and neither was she herself! It felt awfully good to discard that ridiculous role of victim, though; it never had fitted her very well. What had that remark about his family been about? she puzzled, recalling the peculiar comment with a frown. Well, no matter, she had more important things to think about—like what to wear tomorrow night.

Oyster silk was what she finally chose, a simple, slim dress that outlined her supple, slender curves. She fastened a simple gold choker around her throat and found her fingers were trembling.

'Deep breaths,' she said sternly, and then, catching sight of her reflection in the mirror, she laughed aloud. 'First sign of madness,' she observed ruefully. 'Talking to yourself and then replying.'

She stepped back to admire the effect of the gold necklace against her skin and nodded with satisfaction. It was just the right touch. The neckline of the dress emphasised the delicate bone structure of her shoulders and throat, and hinted at the gentle swell of her breasts which were outlined beneath the clinging fabric. She smoothed down the skirt as she slid her feet into a pair of cream court shoes.

Well, he'd better be impressed, she thought, applying a fresh coat of gloss to her lightly tinted lips. When the doorbell rang she picked up the chiffon wrap and handbag from the bed and ran downstairs.

Heart pounding, she looked through the glazed panel at the top of the door and saw the gleam of blond hair. I can do this, she told herself, her lips moving silently in a mantra. I can!

'Hello, Adam.'

'The message on my machine wasn't a joke, then?' He didn't exactly look floored by her sensual beauty, but she tried not to let this daunt her from her purpose. What the hell *is* your purpose, Anna? She ignored this small, troublesome voice in the back of her mind.

'Of course not.' She gave him a radiant smile which

unfortunately didn't decrease the light of suspicion in his eyes. He was dressed in a similar fashion to the first time she'd seen him. He looked more handsome than any man had a right to.

'I'm sorry Mum and Dad can't make it.'

'*Are* you?' One dark brow lifted sceptically as he queried her polite statement.

'Well, if you're going to be pedantic,' she said, exasperated by his total lack of co-operation in her big seduction scene, 'I'm not sorry—at least I *wasn't*,' she muttered darkly.

His lips twitched and a glimmer of humour entered his eyes. 'I was fairly certain that you'd cry off. If you recall we didn't exactly part on the best of terms. Now I get a—' he cleared his throat and his expression made it quite clear her efforts hadn't been *totally* wasted '—warm reception. You're a very confusing woman, Anna Lacey.'

'There's no pleasing some people,' she responded crossly. 'Haven't *you* ever had one of those road-to-Damascus experiences?'

'Sounds interesting,' he said slowly. 'You can tell me all about it later.' He glanced at his wristwatch. 'I've booked a table for eight.' He suddenly leant forward and, bracing one hand against the wall above her head, touched the silky ends of her short hair. He let go and the strands slid back into place. 'Do you polish this stuff?' He was clearly fascinated by this detail of her appearance. 'Come on,' he said abruptly, straightening up. He took her by the elbow and guided her outside to where his car was parked.

Considering Anna had every intention of turning up the heat on their relationship, she was completely flustered by his brief comment. She sank into the leather upholstery and the car purred into life before her breathing returned to anything approaching normality.

'Did I lock the door?' she fretted.

'You did,' he confirmed. 'Did I mention,' he added casually, 'that you look incredibly beautiful tonight?'

'As a matter of fact, no.'

'If I rectify that matter now, am I forgiven?'

'I'll think about it. When a girl goes to this much trouble she expects a little recognition, you know. It took me hours—well, a long time anyway—to get like this. I honestly don't know how Hope copes with looking glamorous permanently. Mind you, she does have better basic ingredients to work with.'

'Probably.' He caught the tail-end of her antagonistic glare before his eyes returned to the road ahead. 'I feel no desire to mess up *her* clothes, though, or play havoc with her hair,' he rasped.

'Then you must be one of the few males under ninety who don't,' Anna responded with far less astringency than she'd intended. Actually she sounded decidedly hoarse.

The idea of Adam fantasising about her was more than enough to send her nervous system into sensory overload. Didn't I begin this evening with the idea I was to be in charge of matters? she asked herself. Naive! she acknowledged in disgust. That's what you are, Anna— naive. Where Adam Deacon is concerned you'll always be dancing to his tune, my girl!

The restaurant attached to the exclusive hotel had a warm and intimate atmosphere. Log fires blazed despite the season, and the French doors were flung open to admit the smell of the summer night and the sound of diners eating alfresco.

'I've never been here before,' she commented after the waiter had smilingly taken their order. 'It's very nice. I can't bear those places where it's so dark you can't see your food.'

'I think subdued light is meant to lend a romantic ambience.'

'I've nothing against candlelight,' she said huskily, her fingers reaching out towards the flickering flames between them.

'I'm pleased to hear it.' He caught one fluttering hand in his and, holding her wide, dilated eyes with his gaze, raised it slowly to his lips. Erotically he touched his open mouth to the palm, sending tingling sensations up her arm. 'I like to see what I'm doing too.'

With the best will in the world there was no way she could have read innocence in his low, gravelly tone and glittering green eyes. A slow, languorous feeling that was in direct contrast to the frantic thud of her heart swept over her.

'You've done it now,' she said with a weak smile. 'I'll never eat anything.'

'Why's that?' Warmth and tender amusement spilled from his eyes, bathing her in a golden glow.

'I've got a lump, right here.' She touched her fingers to the base of her throat where the gold necklace gleamed.

He let go of her hand to touch the spot she indicated. With an expression of fascination he touched the blue-veined point where a pulse beat wildly. 'I'd like to kiss you there, and there, and there, and there...' His finger dropped lower by stages until it rested in the hollow between her breasts.

'*Adam,*' she whispered pleadingly.

'I like it when you say my name.' A savage edge had entered his voice. The angles and planes of his face seemed more pronounced as his eyes returned to her face, and she could see the bands of colour that highlighted the crests of his cheekbones.

'Sir, madam...' They drew apart as the tactful waiter delivered their food.

As she'd predicted, Anna couldn't do the food justice. 'How are the twins?' she asked, trying to introduce some normality to the proceedings.

'Hyperactive. Before you ask, Kate and Jake are also well, but none of them are a subject which particularly interests me at the moment. Did you agree to come out with me because you like my children?'

'No.'

'Then why, Anna? Why are you here?' he persisted. 'What revelation made you say yes? Or is this some act to send me right over the edge?'

'I was miserable not seeing you.' She spoke quickly, with none of the tranquillity she'd practised. 'It seems foolish to…deny. God, I'm doing this all wrong!' she wailed, moving restlessly in her seat. Her darting eyes focused on the exit.

'Calm down.' His voice refocused her attention.

'I think what I'm trying to say is, I'm prepared to compromise,' she said quietly. What had seemed simple when she'd made the decision was suddenly incredibly difficult. She was encouraged by the odd lack of emotion in his own expression. 'You said the best way to exorcise an obsession was to face it.'

A flicker of something that approached anger entered his eyes. 'What if I was wrong…?'

'Surely not,' she responded with a touch of wry humour. 'Adam Deacon, wrong? Isn't that a contradiction in terms?'

'What if it has the opposite effect?' he added, ignoring her gentle taunt.

She gave a wary smile. She was pinning all her hopes on that scenario being true. He *had* to be shown that the awful, predatory Jessica was not the woman for him. She had to let him see that *she* loved him without appearing possessive. It was a delicate balance.

Anna didn't believe it was coincidental that Adam had chosen Jessica. Jessica didn't know him well enough to intrude upon the part of himself he kept private, and that was what Adam wanted. All this precluded Anna making a passionate declaration that would send him running for cover. A simple 'I love you' was definitely a non-starter.

'Is that your way of telling me you've changed your mind? You don't want to be lovers?' She wanted to be his lover for the rest of her life, but there were limits to the amount of honesty she judged he could take.

A spasm of panic corkscrewed through her. She was pinning an awful lot on him finding her irresistible. After all, he had never even once hinted that he felt anything other than lust for her. Aren't you being a little unrealistic? she asked herself. What could a man like Adam Deacon see in you that would make him drastically alter his future? If you want a flower to bloom, she thought determinedly, you have to give it the right conditions.

'You can ask me that?' he breathed incredulously. 'When you take down the barriers, Anna, you do it very thoroughly.'

'Am I going too fast for you?' she enquired innocently. The fierce look he shot her made her inadvertently bite her tongue. 'Ouch,' she cried.

'What's wrong?' he growled in concern.

'I bit my tongue.'

'Don't worry, I'll kiss it better.'

'What are you doing?' she asked in alarm as he got to his feet and took her none too gently by the arm. She dropped her napkin on the floor as he half dragged her from the table.

'I'm taking you to my room. Sorry, didn't I mention I had a room here?' He flashed an insincere smile at the wine waiter as he bustled her past.

'You didn't.'

'Am I going too fast for you?' His honeyed tone was laced with sarcasm.

'The lift...' she protested weakly as he walked straight past it.

'If I get you into a lift I'll make love to you there,

and whilst that would be gratifying I'd prefer a bit more room for manoeuvre.'

'The stairs will be fine,' she gulped, giving a sickly smile. This is what I wanted, isn't it? she thought. She panted to keep up with him as his long legs took the stairs at a breakneck pace.

CHAPTER NINE

'WELL, isn't this nice?' Anna said brightly, looking around the large room.

'Marvellous,' Adam agreed, taking off his jacket and throwing it on the bed. He loosened his tie and flicked on a bedside lamp before switching off the main light.

'Have you stayed here before?'

'Come to me, Anna.' His voice was rich and warm; it made her insides disintegrate and brought a stinging heat to the back of her heavy eyelids.

She slid the high-heeled shoes from her feet and wriggled her free toes in the deep pile of the carpet. 'We didn't eat dinner.' She watched his still figure with an ambiguous mingling of trepidation and longing. 'What will people think?'

'They'll think I've dragged you up here because I couldn't wait another second to make mad, passionate love to you. Before you mention it I think the decor is insipid,' he said smoothly, 'and I don't want to watch television.'

'I wasn't going to say that!' she cried indignantly.

'You weren't so nervous downstairs.'

God, she'd raised his expectations pretty high, she acknowledged with a sinking heart. He was going to expect some expert seductress and what had he got? 'I've not recently...I think I should tell you... Oh, hell,' she cried, wringing her hands.

'Are you trying to tell me you're a virgin?' he joked, expecting the question to lighten the tension she was emanating.

'Not technically,' she said, after giving the question some consideration.

'How can you not *technically* be a virgin?' he asked in an odd, choked voice. It hadn't even crossed his mind that anyone with such unstudied sensuality could be inexperienced. He was shocked, but he also felt a chauvinistic surge of greedy pleasure that he would be the first one. He wasn't going to let a mere *technicality* ruin that prospect. He almost pitied a man who could be thus dismissed.

'I think you might be shocked,' she said with a deep sigh. She cringed from recalling the whole messy episode. It wasn't something she was particularly proud of, but she had been very young at the time and she was inclined to forgive her lapse rather than dwell on the negative aspect.

She had learnt one thing—sex without a deep emotional bond was a barren experience. She was older now and, hopefully, wiser. She'd fallen in love! It was about time she learnt to put the two together.

'I think you'll find I'm difficult to shock,' he observed, studying her pensive face.

'When I was dancing I had this friend. He was…is a dancer, quite famous now. We both joined the company at the same time. We sort of hung out together.' She shot him a swift, half-defiant look from under the sweep of her lashes. 'We were at a party one night and everyone else was paired off. We ended up in bed together. He'd drunk too much and I liked him a lot.'

She closed her eyes and continued in a rush. She didn't want to sound as if she was trying to justify the decision she'd made that night. As decisions went it hadn't been one of her best! The pressure Paul had brought to bear was no excuse in her mind. She could have stopped him if she'd really wanted to.

'If you must know I think I was curious. I mean everyone was always talking about it—sex—and I wanted to know what I was missing. So I'm not a virgin; at least I don't think so.'

'Couldn't you tell?' he asked, watching her with an expression of fascination.

'Well, things went pretty disastrously wrong. It was my fault.' She decided to make a clean breast of the matter. 'I wrecked things.'

'How did you manage that?' he asked with a faint quiver in his voice.

'I laughed. Not a gentle chuckle, but full-blown, helpless, hysterical laughter,' she confessed gloomily. 'At the worst possible moment,' she confided darkly. 'I couldn't help it. The whole thing seemed so ridiculous.' She looked to him for recognition of this fact. 'But he never spoke to me afterwards, which is pretty damned difficult when you have to dance with someone. I thought I'd better warn you that I'm not exactly accomplished.'

There was a long silence. 'Why have you got your eyes closed?' By the sound of his voice he'd come a lot nearer.

Was he *stupid*? 'Because I'm bloody embarrassed,' she hissed from between clenched teeth.

'Do you always tell the truth, Anna?' he asked with laughter in his voice—but it wasn't unkind laughter. She let him take the hand she'd covered her eyes with without a struggle.

'No, I don't,' she admitted honestly. The tip of his tongue flicked across her closed eyelids and a long, sibilant hiss escaped the confines of her dry throat. 'I suppose you're disappointed?' she said, steeling herself for his annoyance. 'A person has to learn some time,' she added defiantly.

'That's indisputable,' he agreed readily. 'I'm amazed you're willing to undergo such a—how did you put it?— ridiculous experience all over again.' He cupped her face in his hands and tilted her chin up towards him.

'I wasn't devastated or emotionally scarred or anything. I just came to the conclusion it was safer to put any spare passion into my dancing,' she told him. 'It was a bit of an anticlimax really. I'd like to think I learned something from it, but that could be wishful thinking. Liking isn't really enough, is it?' She felt her knees buckle as he stroked the side of her face with his forefinger and moved his other hand up and down the length of her spine.

'And you don't *like* me?' Despite his casual tone she could feel his hard muscles rippling with tension.

'Only occasionally.' She licked her dry lips and instigated a meltdown in his green eyes. 'I'm never indifferent to you, though.' As understatements went that was a classic.

'Is that good?' He pulled her pliant body close enough for her to appreciate the urgency of his arousal.

'Not at two in the morning when I can't sleep,' she murmured throatily, allowing her head to fall back as his teeth grazed the base of her throat. A deep moan vibrated in his throat.

'The question is,' he said, raising his chin and staring down into her half-closed eyes, 'can I pass your test, or will you laugh at my efforts?'

'You mean laughter is out completely?' she asked, entering into the spirit of the thing. She widened her eyes with dismay and gave a small shriek as he bent her backwards from the waist and swung her around in a full circle.

'You're amazingly supple.' He lifted her feet clear of the floor and carried her over to the bed. 'It has endless possibilities,' he commented wickedly just before he dropped her unceremoniously onto the well-sprung mattress. She fell back, laughing, but also wondering just how serious he was.

'We'll have to stop that,' he said, joining her. The kiss was an elemental thing, as was the light expression on his face. When he lifted his head she stared at him breathlessly. Her lips felt bruised and swollen and her whole body was throbbing from his touch, aching for him. 'You're not laughing.'

Adam had to impose fierce constraints upon himself not to tear off her clothes and take what she was offering. He'd been deeply moved by her confession. She held nothing back; he'd never known anyone like her. Her darkest secret had only served to emphasise how innocent and vulnerable she really was. Her self-sufficient exterior could be very misleading at times. He was determined to show her what lovemaking could be like.

'I'm not sure I'm breathing,' she gasped faintly.

She touched his chest. The fabric of his shirt was damp with the same sheen of sweat that covered his brow. She could feel the rasp of light hair that covered the muscled hardness. The smell of him in her nostrils was wildly exciting—everything about Adam was exciting. She gave a deep shuddering sigh.

'Oh, you are,' he assured her. 'See?' He placed his hand on her heaving breast to illustrate the point. His fingers curled against her breast where the soft fabric was stretched. Her back arched as he suckled one thrusting nipple through the material. 'I think you're a little overdressed,' he purred. His tongue circled the damp patch left by his mouth, and her fingers curled deeply into his hair. 'Should we get rid of it?'

'Yes, please.' The dress came up over her thighs, and she gave a swift wiggle as he manoeuvred it over her behind, over her raised arms, and the garment hit the opposite wall with a silken slither.

'Dear God!' he breathed raggedly.

She was sitting, he was kneeling, and all he had to do was reach out. Touch me, her eyes screamed, touch me! Her entire body was vibrating with an acute need.

'Do you know when you smile one corner of your mouth goes down, like this?' He touched his thumb to

her mouth. 'I'll never forget the way you smiled at me...
I've tried to. You were laughing at me with your eyes,
such beautiful eyes,' he groaned throatily. 'I couldn't
believe anyone could look so damned sensuous without
trying really hard. I thought, Who the hell does she think
she is? Why does she look so damned pleased with herself when I feel as if I've been poleaxed?'

'I wanted you to laugh with me, Adam, but all you
did was look down your nose at me.'

His nostrils flared as she held out her arms to him.
The gesture was as graceful as every move she made. It
moved him as deeply as a special piece of music or a
beautiful painting, but this work of art inspired him with
a blind, erotic desire. His hands moved to her hips and
his fingers hooked in the waistband of her pants, cut high
on the hip, a silky scrap of material which, along with
the lacey-topped hold-ups, was all she now wore. She
leant forward and wrapped her arms around his neck,
revelling in the strength of his shoulders.

'I wanted to do this then,' he rasped, jerking her to
him, crushing her breasts against his chest. He kissed
her with a fierce desperation, driving all the air from her
lungs. 'I want to stroke every inch of you.' His gaze
dropped to the sway of her breasts. The rosy tips swelled
visibly under his hot scrutiny and he let out a hoarse
gasp before dipping his head to taste the lustrous, soft
flesh. 'Taste every inch of you,' he continued, his husky
voice muffled against her skin.

Anna felt as if she was drowning in the heavy, hot
tide of sensual delight. His skilled hands moved in erotic
arabesques over her spine even as his lips at her breasts
drove her frantic.

'I'd like to taste you,' she admitted huskily.

The half-apologetic comment brought his head up. He
correctly interpreted the desire for reassurance in her
flushed face. 'You don't need to ask permission,' he assured her, his fingers moving to the buttons of his shirt.

'You can do whatever you like,' he promised her throatily.

A thrill of excitement trickled through her trembling body. 'Then let me do that,' she said with a surge of confidence.

She'd expected her fingers to be clumsy, but the remaining buttons melted under her touch. Revelling in her newly discovered power, she pulled the material back from his broad chest. The tension of the muscles in her belly tightened to a painful level. God, but he was beautiful! She slid the shirt off his shoulders and pressed herself against him, luxuriating in the sensation of flesh against flesh. She winced as the buckle of his belt drove into her belly.

'Let me get rid of these,' he said, swinging around to sit on the side of the bed. His back to her, he stepped out of his trousers and then the pants followed suit. His back tapered sharply towards his waist and hips and his buttocks were taut. The muscles that ran smoothly down his thighs flexed and bunched as he took a couple of steps before turning around to face her.

Prepared as she had been for the flagrant image of a man in the grip of primal passion, seeing him still stunned her. Wild thoughts ran through her head. Could it be her own dimensions were not as normal as she'd imagined or was he...?

'I don't think it's possible,' she gasped, staring at him with an awed fascination. 'Could be I'm not adequate for the occasion.' She tried to joke, but her voice was hoarse and weak.

'Do you trust me?' he asked, rejoining her. A musky male scent rose from his heated body. There was a measure of tenderness in the passionate glow of his eyes.

'Yes,' she said, not having to think.

The pleasure and savage satisfaction of her unthinking response were clear to read in his face. 'Touch me,' he commanded, bracing himself above her, almost grazing the quivering flesh of her belly.

She trailed her fingertips over his chest, where the slabs of muscle were sharply delineated, down his flat belly.

'That's right, sweetheart, don't stop...' he encouraged huskily. His hoarse cry encouraged her tentative exploration. Lower lip caught between her teeth, a faint moan emerged at regular intervals from her throat as she felt him respond to her ministrations. When he caught her hand firmly in his and rolled to one side she made a sound of protest.

'I'm not losing you on a technicality this time,' he said, breathing hard.

She gave a breathless laugh even though her earlier doubts had not quite left her. The sound was drowned as his mouth covered her lips. As he moved lower down her body his unerring tongue and hands discovered every vulnerable spot. He told her by word and gesture how beautiful and desirable he found her. When he'd worked his way down the gentle curve of her belly and she thought she'd gone through the whole gamut of possible sensations, he proved her wrong yet again.

'I think we can dispense with these.' The silky pants were discarded, and he knelt between her legs to slowly slide the stockings down over her thighs until her legs too were bare.

There was nothing between them now. The erotic thrill of seeing him kneeling over her drowned out her fear of inadequacy. 'Please, Adam, please,' she pleaded brokenly.

'Not yet.' She could have wept at his firm response. Frustration was gnawing at her; she wanted to feel him, feel him inside her.

His hands were moving over her thighs, gliding over the silky hot skin. She gasped as his tongue tasted the sensitive flesh of her inner thigh. The last remnants of control deserted her as his questing tongue moved higher, following the path his questing fingers had already made to the damp, hot core of her frustration.

She was moaning his name as her body twisted from side to side. It was way beyond anywhere any dream had led her.

The torture stopped as unexpectedly as it had begun. 'I need you, Adam,' she half sobbed.

'I need *you*,' he growled firmly. Kneeling between her parted thighs, he effortlessly lifted her upwards until she faced him sitting across his knees. She felt the thrust of his desire against her lower belly and moved feverishly to increase the contact. She clutched with painful determination at the flesh of his shoulders.

'That's it…' Altering the angle of her body, he slowly and carefully entered her. She opened up like a flower turning to the sun. A series of measured thrusts left her frantic to increase the pressure that brought her such delicious pleasure.

'Is this what you want?' His muscles bunched as he pushed deeper into her receptive moistness to be absorbed by the heat of her.

'Yes!' she screamed triumphantly. Her hands curved around his muscular buttocks and her legs locked around his back as they moved together as one.

The sudden spasm of release was shocking in its strength. She lost all co-ordination as the waves rippled through her. His release swiftly followed her own, and together they fell back onto the bedclothes, which felt cool under their heated flesh.

'Adam…?'

'Mmm?'

'I'm glad you didn't let a technicality ruin that.'

'I'm moderately pleased with myself,' he confirmed smugly, his teeth grazing her shoulder as he burrowed down onto her breasts to fall asleep.

*   *   *

'What do you think you're doing?'

Half in the act of sliding out of bed, Anna stopped. 'I've got to go,' she said softly, leaning over to kiss his shoulder.

'You can't,' he said in a determined voice. He reached for her and she leant away from the touch, sure that if she didn't she'd never get away. It had been hard enough to force herself out of the warm cocoon as it was.

'I must, Adam. It's five-thirty...'

'Five-thirty!' he groaned. He sat up and ran his fingers through his rumpled hair.

'I promised to do the milking this morning,' she admitted ruefully. 'I don't *want* to go.'

'Couldn't you stay a little longer?'

Anna shook her head reluctantly. She longed to accept the husky invitation. 'I can't.'

With a shrug which she found insultingly offhand he accepted this and fell back against the pillows. He put his hands under his head and watched her. Self-consciously she gathered her clothes together and pulled them on.

'You can borrow my toothbrush if you like.'

With a shake of her head she refused this offer. 'I'll manage until I get home.' No doubt there was a right way to deal with the morning after and to leave a man's hotel room with poise and self-assurance, but she didn't know what it was. Thoughts she'd been able to suppress last night refused to be silenced this morning. His next words confirmed her worst fears.

'I've got to go back to London this morning and there're things—'

'Have a good journey,' she interrupted. It was amazing, she reflected, that on the surface she could appear so calm. 'Ring me,' she offered calmly. That was it? That was all he had to say? God, what an idiot I've been! she admonished herself. She could see from the wariness in his eyes he was dreading her making a scene.

What did she expect? A declaration of undying love? Had he ever at any point mentioned love? A *revelation*? No, last night might have been deeply pleasurable for him, but he hadn't broken down and admitted he really loved her. She had to accept that he wasn't going to.

Jessica wasn't about to disappear, because he didn't want her to, she told herself bleakly. It suited Adam this way. The problem is it doesn't suit me, she thought bleakly. At least I tried; I'd never have forgiven myself if I hadn't done that. I don't want to have an affair with you, Adam, she lamented silently. It's too little and too much for me to cope with.

'What, and we'll *do lunch*?' A spasm tightened his features.

'Whatever,' she said casually.

'I think we should work out where we go from here. There are some things I have to tell you. Last night…'

'No!' Panic made her voice sharp. Did he want to officially appoint her the *other woman*? She didn't want to know where she fitted in his life if she didn't have a place in his heart. 'I don't think we have to go anywhere,' she added flatly.

'Anna!' She ignored the sound of his voice as she slammed the door behind her.

'We seem to be ships that pass in the night at the moment,' Charlie Lacey observed as he carried his daughter's case downstairs.

Anna smiled and opened the front door for him. 'I won't be gone long,' she assured him as they walked to her car. She closed the boot after he'd placed her case inside.

'How long?'

'Well, Mrs Morgan is back next week but I'm not sure when Simon will be back, or if.' She was keeping her fingers crossed for him.

'Have you been getting enough sleep whilst we've

been away?' he asked, touching her cheek with one cal-
loused finger.

Anna suddenly felt very close to the tears she'd been
holding at bay all day. 'I'm fine,' she lied cheerfully.

'Thanks for holding the fort until this afternoon. Your
mother did try and ring earlier on to let you know we'd
be late.'

'I must have flicked the "off" switch on the phone
without realising it,' Anna remarked casually. 'At least
you know I haven't been running up an enormous phone
bill.' I'm getting quite good at this lying business, she
thought wryly as she kissed her father goodbye and got
into her car. It had either been ignore the phone completely or switch it off. She just hadn't felt capable of
coping with any communication with Adam just yet. It
could be she never would.

She drove along wrapped in thought. She didn't regret
last night; it had been a deeply special experience for
her and she would treasure the memory for ever. Only
true love could have liberated such feeling in her; she
was confident of that.

Had it been wishful thinking or just stubborn stupidity
to believe that Adam would feel the same way? She
hadn't wanted to pressure him; she'd wanted whatever
he said to be spontaneous. She groaned, recalling the
things she'd said to him in the throes of passion. He
hadn't been fighting against love, just frustrated lust.
She'd been *so* sure he was capable of love—of loving
her!

I have to face the truth, and get on with life. Adam
doesn't love me. But I'm not going to wither and die,
or anything equally pathetic, she told herself firmly. Angrily she wiped the wetness from her cheeks.

At least the time alone house-sitting for Simon would
give her time to think. She didn't have to put on a bright
face for her parents. Her mother had already noticed
something was amiss and all she would need was tender

concern and she would crumble. I don't want to crumble, she thought angrily.

It was six in the morning when a loud hammering downstairs on the post-office door awoke her. She'd only drifted off into an uneasy slumber an hour earlier. Her fatigue-fogged brain tried to concentrate. The noise would wake half the street if she didn't do something about it.

Tying the belt of her robe, she ran down the staircase into the shop. Even through the frosted glass she knew who stood on the other side.

'Go away, Adam!' she yelled as he applied his fist afresh to the wooden panel. 'I'm not going to open this door.'

'Fine, I don't mind conducting this conversation at high volume. I can see net curtains twitching already. I'm sure the neighbours will find it illuminating.'

He would too! 'With any luck someone's already called the police,' she hissed spitefully as she wrestled with the deadlock.

'It's true, then!'

She blinked, taking a step back as he surged into the room, his face livid with rage. 'I could confirm or deny it if you told me *what* is true.'

He gave her a contemptuous look. 'When your father told me where you were I could hardly believe it.' His lips pulled back over tightly clenched teeth.

'My father rarely lies.' She was still trying to make some sense of the outrage he was exuding from every pore. How had she ever thought him unemotional and cool?

Her comment seemed to inflame him further. 'You aren't even going to try and deny it. God, what a fool I've been. A blind idiot. I thought—' He broke off and looked at her with loathing. 'Where is he, then? Hiding under the bed?'

Light dawned—he thought she was here with Simon! He actually imagined... She shook her head incredulously. He wasn't just angry, he was insane.

'Adam, Simon isn't... Will you listen to me and stop pacing about like that? You'll knock something over.' She winced as he narrowly avoided collision with a stack of tinned peaches.

'Listen to you!' he snarled scornfully.

'Unless you want to make a complete fool of yourself that is.' Anger was beginning to stir in her veins, sending the blood surging through her tired brain. The initial satisfaction she'd felt when she knew she was capable of making him jealous was rapidly dissipating. The inconsistency of his feelings bordered on the farcical. He was here, all sweeping condemnation over her supposed liaison with Simon when he had Jessica waiting for him at home.

'It's a bit late for that, isn't it?' he grated. 'To think I actually imagined for one instant that the other night meant something to you. Does he know he's got me to thank for this new, sexually liberated Anna? Shall I tell him? Did you say the same things to him you did to me? Good God, I never thought you could be so cheap! I should have guessed when I saw you in that clinch in the garden.'

Cheap, was she? She felt a dizzying surge of white-hot anger. 'How dare you spy on me? You're so smug, aren't you? It must be nice to be able to look down on us mere mortals from such an Olympian height. How dare you *preach* at me? At least I'm not marrying someone else. You're the only cheat here, Adam.'

'Oh, but I'm not,' he countered. 'That's shocked you, hasn't it? What's wrong, sweetheart? Would you have answered my calls if you'd known I was on the market like your precious Simon? And a much better prospect, if I say so myself. If you'd waited five minutes I'd have told you that morning.'

'It couldn't be that a cheap tart like me made you break off a match made in heaven, could it?' she mocked, swallowing his shocking announcement. Questions crowded into her brain.

'Let's just say I took too much for granted,' he said grimly. A white line of rage outlined his compressed lips as he regarded her with cold disdain. 'To think I thought...' A sound of self-disgust erupted from his chest.

'You thought I might be worthy of you? Am I supposed to be consumed with remorse now?' she asked coldly. 'I've lost my shot at the greatest catch of the century! It might interest you to know that I'm not sharing the bed upstairs with Simon or anyone else. Simon is in Canada patching up his marriage and I am house-sitting. I did try and tell you,' she said as he went deathly pale. 'But you were so eager to rip my character to shreds I couldn't get a word in edgeways.

'No, Adam!' She forestalled his interruption with a raised hand. 'It's my turn now. You've had your say, and it was most instructive. For your information I wouldn't take Jessica's place if you were the only man on the planet! I think you're a narrow-minded, arrogant bore!' The rage burnt itself out abruptly and she suddenly wanted to weep. She wanted to throw herself into his arms and bawl like a baby. She didn't, of course. She stiffened her spine and tilted her chin defiantly.

'I think it only remains for me to say goodbye. You've covered about everything else,' he said austerely. If he felt anything at all it didn't show on his face as he retreated silently out of the door. One flicker of emotion would have been enough to make her break down.

Good riddance, she thought, locking the door firmly. I'm better off without you. Then, despite this self-congratulatory thought, she burst into inconsolable tears.

CHAPTER TEN

'HELP me pin this on, Mum.' Anna took the number she held in her teeth and passed it to her mother along with the pins she held in her fist.

'Turn around, then.' Beth took the large '66' and pinned it to the pink material of the tutu her daughter wore. 'That's it.' She pushed her daughter away to get the full effect of the pink tutu and pale tights offset by football boots and orange stripy socks. 'Very eye-catching, but not exactly aerodynamic, dear.'

'I'm not in this to win, Mum, just to raise lots of lovely money.' Anna pointed to the logo emblazed on her front.

'It's so sad when hospitals need charity to keep them afloat,' Beth sighed.

'I'd argue politics, Mum, but while I'm talking there are probably dozens of kids out there who would benefit from this scanner. The appeal has almost reached the target.'

'Everyone has worked very hard,' Beth agreed.

'Looking out this old outfit made me think of that video Jason made for me,' Anna said casually. 'I couldn't find it anywhere; I don't suppose you…?'

'It must be around somewhere. Goodness me, I do believe you should go and line up now, dear.'

'Mother…' Anna said warningly.

'Well, I lent it to Adam. He seemed so interested in your dancing. I thought he might like to see it,' she rushed on defensively.

'It didn't occur to you I might *not* like him to see it?'

172

'As a matter of fact, no,' Beth said defiantly. 'I think he could be very good for you. He's quite charming.'

'He'd be the first to agree with you,' Anna called over her shoulder as she jogged to the starting line. She was very proud that it had only taken her two weeks to forget the man completely. He was the past, she thought airily, and a past she had no intention of reliving.

The serious runners had already begun. Anna was squashed between a spry octogenarian and a middle-aged man dressed in a giant nappy and nothing else. The atmosphere of the occasion was enough to lift even the most morose of spirits—not that she needed cheering up.

'First mile's the worst,' a large Easter bunny commented as she topped the first incline.

'That's what you need—limitless optimism,' Anna laughed breathlessly. 'Can you breathe in that thing?' she asked, when half a mile further along the rabbit was still keeping pace with her. She eyed the heavy costume and wondered how the poor idiot in it could see. It must be stifling under all those layers of fur and padding.

'I might need resuscitation,' the muffled voice observed.

'You could take the head off,' Anna suggested. A stitch knifed into her side; laughing and running didn't make for comfort.

'Later.'

Anna shrugged and offered her collection tin to the spectators lining the route. She accepted the juice offered around the next bend and once more found the rabbit at her elbow.

'Have you done one of these before?' she yelled. He really did appear to be having trouble.

'No, you?'

'Two other half marathons and one marathon, but I'm not fit enough to do one of those right now.'

'Fit! You mean you train for these things?'

Anna was beginning to feel concerned about the rabbit. Enthusiasm was all very well, but in this heat, in that outfit, if he wasn't super-fit he was in real trouble.

'Didn't you train?'

'Spur-of-the-moment thing.' He was panting pretty badly.

'You should take some fluids.'

'Can't drink in this thing.'

'Anna!' Two nuns with beards ran past and playfully slapped her behind. 'Great outfit, love!'

'Friends?' the rabbit enquired.

'Rugby players; one of them comes to me for massage.'

'I might need some of that before this is over.'

'You can always drop out.'

'And lose my sponsorship money? I'm running for the scanner appeal too. Don't wait for me,' the muffled voice added heroically as Anna adapted her pace to her lumbering running partner's. 'I'll get there eventually. Remember the tortoise and the hare.'

'I think you're in the wrong outfit for that analogy.'

The next several miles passed in relative silence if you didn't count the gasps and groans coming from the large figure beside Anna. She'd just decided that he couldn't be that unfit to keep up this pace when the Easter bunny staggered in front of her and fell dramatically at her feet.

'Oh, no!' she groaned, coming to a halt in front of the prone figure. She dropped to her knees. 'I'll get you out of this in a minute. Get the first-aid people,' she yelled to the small group which had gathered around. 'I think this thing is stuck,' she gasped, struggling with the rabbit head. I hope the poor man is breathing in there, she thought, panting.

The thick fur fabric made it impossible for her to find a pulse. The head shot off suddenly, throwing her back on her heels. 'Are you al…?' she began. 'You rat!' she spat venomously, much to the amazement of several people who'd stopped to assist. She stiffened with a fierce sense of outrage. Was this some twisted joke?

'Rabbit, Anna, rabbit,' Adam Deacon corrected her firmly.

He wasn't even breathing hard. He actually looked in a much better condition than she did. 'That was quite an act,' she yelled wrathfully. 'It's some comfort that you look a total fool.' So much for his much revered dignity.

'I was hoping you'd notice that. Hold on, Anna, wait for me!' he cried as she sped off.

She was fit, but he was obviously fitter. No matter how hard she tried to shake him off he stuck firmly to her side.

'That's right, take some fluids,' he said approvingly when she raised a beaker to her lips.

With a squeak of frustration she flung her half-full cup at his head. 'Can't you take a hint? I don't want you.'

'Yes, you do, and I'm not going to go away until you admit it.'

'Are you mad?' Red-faced, she shot him an incredulous look.

'Just *desperate*. This was the only way I could be sure of getting you to talk to me. I knew you'd never quit once you'd started.'

'I'm so predictable, am I?'

What the hell was he doing here? Was this some bizarre joke? He couldn't mean what his words suggested. Anna couldn't permit herself the luxury of hope. The memory of the fall from optimism to despair was still painfully fresh in her mind.

'You've got something that belongs to me.' She threw him a hard-eyed scowl. 'Mum had no right to let you have it; it's private.'

I'm over him, I'm coping—that's hysterically funny! she thought confusedly. Who am I fooling? Anna almost stumbled and Adam's hand shot out. She ignored it and his injured expression. Now wasn't the time to start holding hands; just seeing him was a specialised form of torture!

'Beth told you?'

'Jessica told me.'

'Jessica!' That had surprised him; she could tell from his voice.

'Girlish confidences,' she continued in a soft, taunting voice. 'You know how it is.'

'I'm happy to say I don't.'

'I'd be interested to hear what you thought of my performance,' she gasped as her oxygen-hungry lungs greedily absorbed all she could supply.

'That makes a nice change,' he growled sarcastically. 'You've assiduously avoided hearing anything I've had to say till now. When was the last time you answered a phone? Your poor mother is running out of excuses to cover your reluctance to talk to me.'

'You and my mother have a regular mutual appreciation society.'

'I hadn't realised just how much you'd lost until I saw that tape,' he said abruptly. 'Someone with less guts and determination would have been permanently maimed emotionally. You haven't wasted your time wailing about the hand fate dealt you, you've got on with your life. The fact you can wear that thing—' he reached out and touched the skirt of her tutu '—as a joke impresses me more than I can say. It says it all—you're quite a woman, Anna.'

She couldn't mistake the sincerity in his deep tone, and tears stung her eyelids. 'Did Mum tell you about today?'

She couldn't risk looking at him. She might see what she wanted to in his eyes, not what was really there. One foot in front of the other; that was what she had to concentrate on.

'I'm not going to reveal my sources. I knew you wouldn't speak to me voluntarily. Surely you didn't think the moody silence would make me go meekly away?' He sounded incredulous at the notion.

He was so unbearably sure of himself, it made her want to scream. But all her breath was needed to keep up the killing pace which was fast reducing her to a wreck. At least the pain was distracting enough to enable her to stay relatively sane in his company.

'Why the pantomime?' she snapped.

'I thought you'd be glad I'm prepared to make a complete fool of myself for you, not to mention a good cause.'

'All this is meant to impress *me*! This...this circus?' she spluttered.

'I'm just entering into the spirit of the thing. Let's face it, I couldn't make a bigger fool of myself than I did that morning. Besides, there's nowhere for you to hide from me here.'

She only lost her rhythm for a second. There never had been anywhere for her to hide from him. Despite the confidence and determination in his voice she glimpsed uncertainty etched in the lines of his face.

'You won't have any arguments on that subject from me. You're a fool, Adam.' Adam was apologising—she couldn't believe it, but if he wanted to say something he would have to spell it out clearly.

'I hate being told what to do, Anna—'

'You don't say,' she snorted.

'For God's sake, woman, let me finish. I really thought I was doing the right thing when I got engaged to Jessica. The fact my entire family made it clear they didn't agree made me dig my heels in. I didn't want to admit they were right.

'Even if I hadn't met you I don't think I'd have gone through with it,' he confessed. 'I felt a complete swine! As far as I was concerned Jessica was the one prepared to make all the sacrifices and I was going to throw it all in her face. It was my fault for rushing into the engagement. After Ben and Tessa's death I should have taken time out before I made any decisions, but I didn't. Angus Montford meant a lot to me, and although it might seem bizarre I felt as if it was him I would be betraying.

'For God's sake, Anna, if you don't slow up you'll never reach the finish line.'

'I don't like being told what to do either.' The arm that hooked around her waist brought her to an abrupt halt. 'How dare—?'

A firm kiss silenced her protest as he lifted her clear off the ground. A ripple of applause broke out as runners ran around the obstacle of a ballerina in football boots being ruthlessly kissed by a six-foot-plus rabbit. An enterprising young local took a snap which would end up on the pages of a national daily and launch him into a new career.

'Adam, people are staring!' Dazed, she clutched at him as her shaking knees threatened to buckle beneath her.

'Let them,' he said carelessly.

'I thought you had to be careful of your reputation.' The possessive gleam in his eyes was making her heart thud.

'I'd have the reputation of being the biggest fool in history if I let you go. I love you, Anna.'

'You loved Jessica,' she reminded him. His simple statement had made her nearly explode with joy.

'Never,' he said with a hint of impatience. 'You knew that, Jessica knew that. I had told her long before we spent the night together that it was over. I had every intention of telling you just that, but your own agenda that night did sort of divert me,' he reflected.

She blushed as she recalled how cold—no, *hot*-bloodedly she'd set out to seduce him. 'Marrying someone you don't love is an awful thing to do.'

'I'm a reformed man,' he announced. The humble statement was spoilt by the dangerous gleam in his eyes.

'But if it's any comfort my blue eyes were never the main attraction for Jessica. She played on my gratitude to her stepfather right from the beginning, and I was too blind to see it. She became angry enough to admit she had never really cared for Angus at all. In fact she was furious that he'd left part of his estate to set up a charity devoted to medical research. I am a director of the charity, and it seems early on she had a notion that she might be able to break the trust.

'As for the job she sacrificed, it was never hers to refuse.' His lips twisted in a cynical grimace. 'Jessica is incredibly ambitious and seeing the job she'd spent the last two years grafting to get go to someone else must have been agony. For some reason she decided to transfer her energies to getting me. This probably sounds conceited, but it explains why she was so understanding when I told her how I was feeling about you.

'I really expected her to see what had become so glaringly obvious to me—that we were totally unsuited. That was why I tried to throw her together with the children that weekend, but mumps and my mother intervened. At the time it seemed kinder to let her be the one to call things off.'

'They're green,' Anna corrected him. 'Your eyes are green.' She was still trying to take in these revelations. Jessica's visit to her had obviously been motivated by pure malice. She couldn't have Adam and she'd wanted to make sure no one else did either.

'You noticed,' he said with a pleased grin.

'The way you glare at me, it would have been hard to miss. You said some awful things to me.'

'I did think you'd left my bed to jump into someone else's. I'm normally the mildest of creatures. Remember this was the same guy you'd had some mawkish adolescent crush on and the same guy whom I'd seen kissing you in the garden. I should have done what my instincts told me to at the time,' he observed grimly.

She didn't enquire what this had been; his clenched fists sort of gave the game away. 'You didn't trust me.'

He ripped off his gloves and took her chin in his hand. 'That morning after hadn't gone exactly as I'd planned,' he explained drily. 'I was all pumped up to pledge my eternal love—something I've had little practice at. I wanted to tell you that it was all off between Jessica and me, and you proceeded to act as if we'd done nothing more intimate than shake hands. ''Casual'' doesn't even begin to describe your behaviour. I thought you'd succeeded in exorcising your obsession.'

'It was you who said that,' she reminded him.

'I was clutching at straws at the time, Anna. I'd never had cause to call my integrity into question before I met you. Learning love is stronger than pride was a hard lesson.'

'What about during our night together?' she enquired huskily. His voice might have contained a wry note of humour when he'd spoken of love, but there was nothing humorous about the deep sincerity in his eyes. 'I just about exhausted the dictionary definitions of love that night. You didn't say a word.'

'People say things they don't mean in the throes of passion.'

'I don't.' Adam caught his breath at the expression in her eyes as she made the admission.

'I couldn't be sure of that at the time,' he said, holding her gaze steadily. 'That's why I waited. I didn't want any misunderstandings about what I wanted to say. Unfortunately I couldn't compete with the cows.' His smile carried the shadow of recent pain.

'I thought you wanted it casual, Adam. You hadn't said anything and as far as I was concerned you were marrying Jessica. I had no right to demand anything you weren't going to give freely. It's just that loving you felt so *right*, Adam.' A husky catch throbbed in her low, passionate voice. 'I couldn't let you marry Jessica without trying to show you how much I loved you. I thought I'd made a terrible mistake and you didn't feel the same way. I didn't want to be your mistress, Adam.'

He called her an extremely rude name and his fingers tightened on her upper arms.

'If you really loved me, you wouldn't be so rude.'

'I don't expect marriage to you to be a smooth ride.'

'Is that a proposal?' She tried to look shocked and disapproving, but she could feel an idiotic grin on her face. So much for being mysterious and hard to get!

'I've taken advice from my family…'

'Adam, I won't marry you just because the children like me,' she said, a cloud passing over her shining joy. Uncertainty made her lips quiver slightly.

'Kate tells me neither she nor Jake are children. My darling Anna, if the children hated you I wouldn't give a damn. Mind you, it makes life easier that they don't,' he felt compelled to admit. 'You haven't given me an answer yet. Is it because of the ready-made family?'

'Not at all.' She nipped that stupid notion in the bud. 'They're much easier to get on with than you.'

'Then say it, Anna! Say "I love you, Adam, and I'll marry you".'

'This is coercion,' she told him with mock severity.

'This is two weeks of pure hell talking, Anna,' he said seriously. 'I'm not letting you go until I know you're mine.'

Anna could have pointed out the impractical nature of this assertion, but she didn't. 'I've been so miserable,' she cried, surging forward and flinging her arms enthusiastically about his neck. 'You're the only man I've ever seduced and the only man I've ever loved.' Her brown eyes glowed as he lifted her up to face level.

'You're the only woman I've ever dressed up as an Easter bunny for,' he admitted. 'It's not the first time I've made a fool of myself, though it's probably the most public. I had made my mind up never to repeat the experience after that awful morning. Only there's something very infectious about your recklessness. You've let me look at the world through your eyes, and you know something? It's really not such a bad place, so long as you're in it.'

'Don't be so *nice,*' she gulped urgently. 'Or I'm going to cry!' she warned.

He looked at her wet lashes with tender astonishment. 'I'll never understand women.'

'That's obvious,' she sniffed, 'or you wouldn't have got engaged to Jessica. When she warned me off—'

'You're never going to let me forget that, are you?' he interrupted her. An attentive expression abruptly stole over his face. 'Warned you off?'

'She paid me a little visit, and I'm not telling you what I said because it will only confirm your opinion that I'm a shameless hussy. Besides, you're big-headed enough without women fighting over you. If I'd been Hope I'd have laid her out cold,' she told him a tinge wistfully. 'Her temper bypasses her brain and goes straight to her fists.'

'What sort of family have I got myself mixed up with?' he said mournfully. His eyes darkened with passion as she laughed up at him. 'God, but I want to make love to you,' he said.

'In that case,' she replied, casting him a sultry smile that sent his pulses racing, 'it might be a good idea to finish this race.'

Some time later, holding hands, they stepped over the finish line together.

'Not your best time, Anna,' a group of fellow fundraisers teased. They eyed Adam with overt curiosity.

'My fault, I'm afraid,' Adam said, his smile widening as he saw Anna's blush deepen. 'I needed nursing.'

'There you are, Adam.' A voice Anna vaguely recognised averted his attention.

'Mother, what are you doing here?' Adam's voice

held a note of resignation as he turned to face the tall, elegant woman for whom the crowds parted.

Anna stared. This couldn't be the frail old lady she'd spoken to on the phone. Elderly she might be, but this woman looked the picture of health. Her posture was elegant and erect, and her clothes had an unmistakable designer quality.

'I came to see you compete, darling. I always came to see you and Benedict on sports day.'

'I suppose you're too old to stop listening at key-holes?'

'I'd never resort to anything so vulgar, Adam. Aren't you going to introduce me to your charming friend? I rather think we've spoken before. Anna? I was aching to meet a woman who could make my painfully proper son dress up in a bunny outfit.'

'How did you...?' Adam began.

His mother gave him a superior smile. 'When one has a son who is secretive and uncooperative in the extreme, one has to be resourceful.'

Anna smiled shyly. 'Mrs Deacon?' The elder woman's eyes were on the hand still firmly enclosed in Adam's. Anna tried to disentangle her fingers, but Adam resisted her efforts.

'Actually, it's Arnold, but do call me Sara—or Mother?' She threw a challenging look in Adam's direction. 'Don't glare so. Can you blame me for being so relieved to see you with someone nice after that harpy? Considering how undemonstrative you can be holding hands is tantamount to a public declaration of love.

'Don't you find him a little reserved?' she asked Anna curiously. 'I was going to say stuffy, but...' She smiled and Adam gave a philosophical shrug. 'The boys didn't want to change their name when I married Gerald,' she explained to Anna.

'Anna's looking a little shocked because she was expecting a weak, fragile, grey-haired old lady. I believe

you gave an Oscar-winning performance over the telephone.'

'I was very concerned at the time. You can hardly
blame me for taking advantage of the circumstances.'

'He's apt to do that himself,' Anna commented.

'Precisely,' Sara Arnold said, bestowing an approving
smile on Anna. 'I do have grey hair, Adam.' She raised
her hand to her perfectly coiffed hair. 'And I am sev-
enty-five. I was forty when Adam was born, Anna; he
was a very troublesome baby. I'll be so relieved when
he settles; I've had nothing but worry for thirty-five
years.'

'How did you get here, Mother?' he asked casually.
'By bus? Or did you decide to wheel out the chauffeur
and Rolls today? My mother, Anna, is the widow of
Gerald Arnold—*the* Arnold of Arnold frozen foods.'

Anna's brain was whirling; the food chain was a
nationwide operation. 'Does that mean you're rich?' she
asked with some dismay.

'My stepfather left Ben and me a large chunk of
shares in his will,' he admitted with a shade of embarrassment.

'And Adam and the children will get the rest when I
die.'

'As you can see,' Adam drawled sarcastically, 'that
could be any moment.' He exchanged a dry smile with
his parent. 'It injures my male pride no end to have to
admit that Jessica, it transpired, was more in love with
my prospects than me. She had a lot of ideas about how
she'd like to spend my fortune. That's why she was so
willing to put up with the inconvenience of children, not
to mention the fact that I was in love with someone else.

'You don't know what a relief it was when I realised
she didn't want me for my body, or even my mind, but
my bank balance! Mother, could you give us a few
minutes alone?' He spoke curtly enough to bring a frown
of protest to Anna's smooth brow. 'I'll try and persuade

Anna to forgive your manipulative machinations; only a truly heartless woman would exploit her grandchildren's illness.'

'That was rude,' Anna said, watching the elderly woman move away, leaning slightly on a silver-topped cane.

'When you get to know my mother better you'll appreciate that subtlety doesn't work. Trust me on this one,' he advised her with a wry smile. 'Come and sit over here.' He drew her over to one of the benches that lined the finishing area.

'I want you to have no doubts about Jessica,' he said gravely, his eyes examining her face with so much tenderness that Anna felt as if her heart would explode with pure joy.

'The only reason we lasted as long as we did,' he continued, 'was that we never did discover anything about each other. Our relationship was always superficial and selfish—mutually so,' he confessed. 'I'd given up on love a long time before. Ben had been the lucky one. I'd come to the conclusion he and Tess were exceptions.

'Then you came along and turned my whole world upside down. I was lost the first time I laid eyes on you, Anna. Every objection I tried to place between me and the way I felt kept disintegrating the more I saw of you, the more I got to know you.

'I thought Jessica genuinely cared about me. I didn't want to humiliate her. I was confidently expecting her to be ready to throw in the towel when things were obviously going wrong. The weekend was meant to push things in the right direction. Jessica is fond of her creature comforts.'

'That's despicable!' Anna told him solemnly. 'Not to mention devious.' Happiness was spiralling out of control in her heart.

'Thank you,' he said, outrageously. 'It was frustrating to find all that forward planning had gone to waste.

Then, not long afterwards, I learnt from a few things she let slip that she was *very* interested in my financial affairs. After that things fell into place.' He gave a cynical smile. 'It was easy to say goodbye in the end.'

'Why didn't you tell me about the money?'

'I suppose you want me to give everything away to a shelter for three-legged, agoraphobic gerbils from broken homes?' He teased a smile from her suddenly solemn face. 'To be honest, Anna, I don't dwell too much on my great expectations. I may not be in my stepfather's league but I'm financially stable. Gerald was a great guy, but I've not got the same taste for ostentation that he had.'

'Were you worried I was a gold-digger too?'

'Is that what's bothering you?' He laughed incredulously. 'Listen here, Anna,' he said, taking her face between his hands and pressing his nose up to hers. 'You've really got the most amazing eyes I've ever... What was I saying?' he asked vaguely, his eyes sinking to her mouth. 'Your avaricious soul, wasn't it? Can we be serious for one moment here, darling? You're the most unworldly creature ever to draw breath. You're not going to tell me you've got some idealistic objection to marrying a rich man?'

'And if I did?' she said, catching the tip of her tongue between her teeth. 'Would you give it all away?'

He caught the twinkle in her eyes as she relaxed and gave in to the temptation of her slightly parted lips. 'I can see you're one of those women who want to change a man.'

'You're not perfect,' she told him, 'but the thing is I sort of like you like that.' She never had been very good at hiding her feelings, and it was such a relief to be able to let her love shine forth. 'It's been the most miserable two weeks of my life, Adam,' she told him frankly. 'Can you think of any therapy to help me recover from the trauma?'

Adam rose to the challenge.

'Wow!' she said, gasping for air as he lifted his head a few minutes later.

'Wow!' he teased, running a finger along the curve of her jaw and nuzzling the pulse-point at the base of her throat.

'Did you hire this outfit?'

He nodded and looked puzzled.

'You've lost your mind.'

'That happened weeks ago,' he explained. 'I've got used to the idea now.'

London's streets aren't just paved with gold—they're home to three of the world's most eligible bachelors!

You can meet these gorgeous men, and the women who steal their hearts, in:

NOTTING HILL GROOMS

Look out for these tantalizing romances set in London's exclusive Notting Hill, written by highly acclaimed authors who, between them, have sold more than 35 million books worldwide!

Irresistible Temptation by Sara Craven
Harlequin Presents® #2077
On sale December 1999

Reform of the Playboy by Mary Lyons
Harlequin Presents® #2083
On sale January 2000

The Millionaire Affair by Sophie Weston
Harlequin Presents® #2089
On sale February 2000

Available wherever Harlequin books are sold.

HARLEQUIN®
Makes any time special ™

Visit us at www.romance.net

HPNHG